James Philip

––––––––––

The Road to Berlin

––––––––––

UNTIL THE NIGHT – BOOK TWO

Cover concept by James Philip
Graphic Design by Beastleigh Web Design

———————

The Bomber War Series

Book 1: Until the Night
Book 2: The Painter
Book 3: The Cloud Walkers

Until the Night Series

A serialisation of Book 1: Until the Night in five parts

Part 1: Main Force Country – September 1943
Part 2: The Road to Berlin – October 1943
Part 3: The Big City – November 1943
Part 4: When Winter Comes – December 1943
Part 5: After Midnight – January 1944

The Road to Berlin

———————————

We are going to scourge the Third Reich from end to end. We are bombing Germany city by city and ever more terribly in order to make it impossible for her to go on with the war. That is our object; we shall pursue it relentlessly.

War is a nasty, dirty, rotten business. It's all right for the Navy to blockade a city, to starve the inhabitants to death. But there is something wrong, not nice, about bombing that city.

Air Marshall Sir Arthur Harris
[Air Officer Commanding-in-Chief RAF Bomber Command]

Chapter 1

Friday 1st October, 1943
RAF Ansham Wolds, Lincolnshire

Two nights ago 350 Lancasters and Halifaxes had attacked Bochum in the Ruhr, wrecking the town from end to end at a cost of only 9 heavies. Now, probably because of the unusually low casualty rate on the Bochum raid, the AOC had conditionally reinstated No 647 Squadron's operational status and ordered Ansham Wolds to bring to readiness 8 aircraft for operations that night.

The morning was dull, wet and dismal but none of that mattered.

Adam was back at the controls of a Lancaster, B-Baker and reunited with his crew of incorrigible old lags. All was well with the world. Ben had nudged him in the ribs before they mounted up.

"There's no need to look so bloody cheerful, Skipper!"

The forecast was for a dry clear night but that afternoon the rain came and went across the high Lincolnshire Wold beneath a leaden overcast. Adam focussed on the job in hand. Although this was only a test flight, there was no room for sloppiness, no excuse for complacency.

"Let's get on with it, Ted," he decided, half-turning in the bucket seat to address Flying Officer Edward Hallowes, his flight engineer. Hallowes had joined the crew in July, flown 12 ops with him and 17 in total.

"Roger, Skipper!" Acknowledged the other man, poker-faced. In March, 5 ops into his tour Ted's previous pilot had misjudged a landing coming back from Nuremburg. The crash had killed three crew members and put the other four in hospital. To this day Hallowes had no recollection of the actual crash, only of waking up in hospital the next day. It was his twenty-third birthday in a week or so. Ted Hallowes was overly fastidious, fussy in his personal habits and the butt of a good many practical jokes.

When Bomber Command had discontinued the employment of second pilots, flight engineers had taken over many of their functions. It was not uncommon to find an engineer with pilot's time in his logbook, and Ted Hallowes was one such. Having gone solo on a single-engine biplane trainer – a Tiger Moth - he had fallen by the wayside on multi-engine aircraft and opted to transfer to his present trade. During cross country navigation exercises and long training flights Adam occasionally invited Ted Hallowes to take the controls. In an emergency - if Adam was hit - Ted might be able to hold the heavy steady long enough for the others to bale out...

"Switches off! SWITCHES OFF!"

"Inner tanks on...INNER TANKS ON!"

"Immersed pumps on...IMMERSED PUMPS ARE ON, SKIPPER!"

"Check seat secure! CHECKED SECURE."

"Brakes on and pressure up? BRAKES ON AND PRESSURE IS OK!"

"Undercarriage locked...LOCKED!"

Next the engine controls checks.

"Master engine cocks! OFF!"

"Throttles! HALF-INCH OPEN!"

"Prop controls? FULLY UP!"

"Slow-running cut-out switches...SET TO IDLE CUT-OFF."

"Supercharger controls...M RATIO."

"Warning light...NO WARNING LIGHT SHOWING."

"Air intake heat control...READS COLD."

"Radiator shutters...RAD SHUTTER OVER-RIDE SWITCHES ARE SET TO AUTOMATIC, SKIPPER."

It was the Lancaster pilot's catechism. Adam used to boast he could call down the check list in his sleep, until that was a friend had mentioned, in passing that: *'Actually, old man, you've been known to do just that!'*

"Prepare to start up."

"OK. We're ready to start up, Skipper!"

"Tank selector cock...TURNED TO NUMBER TWO TANK."

"Master engine cock on...ON. Booster pump...ON."

B-Baker was new from the factory. The aircraft smelled new, felt new, and gleamed all over. Adam slid back the cockpit window and signalled to the erks manning the battery cart. An arm waved back.

"Contact starboard-inner!" Adam shouted, flicking the cover off the starter button and jamming it hard into its socket. Instantly, grey-blue smoke shot through with a spurt of crimson flame belched from the exhausts of the Merlin. The starboard-inner was started first on Lancaster Mark Is and IIIs: it powered the Heywood compressor which ran the aircraft's pneumatic system. The engine turned, once, twice then faster than a man could count. After perhaps a dozen turns the Merlin ran true, awesomely, magnificently true. B-Baker hummed with the power of that one engine, airframe reverberating softly.

"Slow-running cut-out control!"

"SET TO ENGINE-RUNNING POSITION!" Hallowes yelled above the smooth, murderous roar of the Merlin.

Within five minutes all four of B-Baker's Merlins were firing.

Adam disengaged the booster coil switch and the aircraft ran on its own power, independent of the ground. The thunder of the Merlins always concentrated his mind. Lately, it seemed the only time he was ever really at peace with himself was when he was locked within their earth-shattering, deafening circle.

Turning the ground/flight switch to FLIGHT Adam waved away the ground crew, watched the erks wheel the battery cart clear of the Lancaster, and devoted his attention to the Merlins. Slowly opening each up to 1,200 revs he attuned his ear to their brutal heartbeat. Detecting nothing untoward he let the engines idle, warming. Oil temperatures needed to be around 15 degrees centigrade and coolant temperatures at least 40 degrees before they continued the engine checks. He and Hallowes embarked on the next series of checks while they waited.

"D.R. Compass...ON AND SET, SKIPPER!"

Adam's eyes swept across his instruments. He checked a second time, then once more. Only a fool tempted providence. Familiarity bred carelessness and in this business, carelessness was as deadly as a night fighter's cannons. He raised and lowered the flaps to test the hydraulic system, eyed the rising engine temperatures. In succession he turned off each Merlin's electric booster pump to confirm that the engine-driven pumps were functioning correctly. B-Baker continued to pass every test with flying colours.

"Rad shutters...OVER-RIDE SWITCHES SET AT OPEN!"

Hallowes leaned over his pilot to assist with the two-speed supercharger checks. The control was only usually set in "S", or *supercharged*, ratio at heights above twelve thousand feet. Above this altitude a Merlin needed supercharging - or *'blowing'* - to ensure that sufficient air was 'blown' into it to achieve the correct air to fuel ratio. Without supercharging engine performance rapidly degraded above this altitude. Conversely, setting the control to "S" ratio at ground level was supposed to make the revs fall. The test went without mishap, and wordlessly, both men concentrated on the constant-speed propeller controls. With the control down the revs dropped in copybook fashion. Next, Hallowes eased the throttles hard up against the stops while his pilot checked boost and revs prior to throttling back down to 3,000 revs at nine pounds of boost. None of the propellers was constant speeding.

Lastly, came the magneto tests.

Each Merlin had twin magnetos and spark plugs for its twelve cylinders. When one magneto was switched off the manual stated that the resulting 'magneto drop' on a healthy engine should never exceed 100 revs. A cack-handed or a weak-kneed pilot could easily manufacture an excessive mag drop. Adam tended to be obsessively cautious when carrying out magneto tests. Even he had been known to inadvertently 'oil up' the plugs. A 'mag drop' of over 150 revs usually meant one of three things: the plugs were dirty, that is, oiled up; or the gap between the contact breaker points needed resetting; or that the points were sticking. Adam identified a borderline mag drop on the starboard outer Merlin. He repeated the test and the drop stubbornly remained borderline. He shrugged it off.

"Must be the dial, Ted. Write it down for checking when we get back." The intercom crackled as Adam called around the crew stations, visualising each man at his position as his voice broke through the hissing static. "Pilot to bomb-aimer. Talk to me, Angus!"

"Bomb-aimer to Pilot," returned the solemn Highland tones of his bomb-aimer from Inverness. Two years ago Flying Officer Angus 'Round Again' Robertson had been a bank clerk. A quiet youngster with freckles and a mop of unruly black hair he barely looked seventeen despite the fact his birth certificate showed he had enjoyed his twenty-second birthday in August.

'You worked in a bank? More than enough to make a chap volunteer for flying duties?' Adam had suggested, attempting to put the boy at his ease on their first meeting. Angus's brow had furrowed. Irony was not his strong point. Nor initially, was his instinct for survival. Over Cologne in the first week of July, with one Merlin feathered and night fighters everywhere, the young Scot had come on the intercom and complained that he was unsure which ground markers to bomb.

'Bomb the nearest green spot markers!' Adam had retorted, incredulously.

There had been a short delay. Then, doggedly: 'Bomb-aimer to pilot.'

'What?'

'There are green TIs all over the shop, Skipper.'

Up ahead a Lancaster took a direct hit and exploded, its fuel, cookie and incendiaries lighting up in an incandescent bubble of orange and crimson death. All around searchlights hunted for prey. Blue-tinged radar-predicted masters flicking this way and that, white slaves tracked aimlessly, waving from side to side waiting for the masters to lock onto new prey.

'Can we go round again, Skipper?' Momentarily, Adam had been lost for words. Plaintively, Angus had repeated his request: 'Bomb-aimer to pilot. Can we go round again, please?'

Spent shrapnel had rattled evilly against the cockpit windows.

'No we bloody well can't! Find a green TI and drop the bombs on it! Do it now! That's an order!'

Adam still shivered whenever he thought about that night. It was one of those ill-starred ops on which they could very, very easily have all got killed. Most ops had the odd dicey moment, you got used to that. But that Cologne raid was dicey from take off to landing, a nightmare. Safely back on the ground he had taken the young Scot by the arm, led him out of earshot of the rest of the crew.

'Don't you ever do that again, Angus! This work is bloody dangerous and the last thing we need is somebody going out of their way to make it any more dangerous! Savvy?'

Round Again had got the idea after that. There was a time to be keen and there was a time to be circumspect. Over a well-defended, murderous place like Cologne you did the business and you ran like hell.

The old man of the crew was Flight Sergeant Arthur 'Bert' Pound, at thirty four, like thirty-two year old Ben Hardiman, decidedly long in the tooth by aircrew standards, married with three young boys. Bert had come to Bomber Command via a working life spent in a Sheffield steel foundry. He was fifteen trips into his second Lancaster tour. Bert was B-Baker's W/T operator and his position was immediately forward of the main spar on the port side of the aircraft. Wireless operators on Lancasters enjoyed the dubious privilege of sitting beside the hot air vent. While everybody else gradually froze, despite their new-fangled electrically heated flying suits, Bert broiled.

Navigators on Lancasters were sandwiched behind the pilot's high-backed armoured seat and the W/T operator's station. A narrow 'walkway' – no more than an equipment obstructed gap - ran along the starboard side of the fuselage. This was where the flight engineer had his post, with his control board bolted onto the right-hand side of the cockpit.

Immediately to the right of the pilot was a fold-down seat the engineer used when he was required to help the pilot fly the aircraft, for example, at take-offs and landings or whenever an extra pair of eyes was needed in the cockpit.

The two gunners were tucked up in their turrets.

Adam had a soft spot for his gunners.

Others called it a blind spot and regarded what he characterized as 'licence', as 'indulgence'. He did not care. In his book air gunners were a breed apart. Frostbite, loneliness, claustrophobia, cramp and boredom interspersed with split seconds of visceral feral terror represented the gunner's lot, and through everything he had to stay alert because his eyes and his split-second reflexes were all that stood between the life or death of his crew. In the blackness of the night a fighter was no more than a smudge in a gunner's eye, a dim mote against a dark background. A mote in a gunner's eye in the inky darkness of the German night was all the warning a gunner ever got of an attacking fighter. That and a burst of cannon fire.

The mid-upper gunner was a lanky, spotty nineteen-year-old from Taunton who was revelling in his transition from farmhand to air gunner. To all outward appearances, Flight-Sergeant Bob Marshall was utterly fearless. Moreover, Bob had recently discovered girls. This and the fact that seven weeks ago he had become a permanent member of the Wingco's crew had made Bob's contentment complete. He was a big kid, immature even for his few years, but it mattered not one iota to his pilot because the boy was a damnably good gunner.

The tail gunner, Flight-Sergeant Max 'Taffy' Davies was a wiry twenty-four year old former miner from Merthyr Tydfil in South Wales. Currently, he was sporting a black eye and a bruised face from a recent altercation, allegedly, with a pair of brown types in Lincoln. Two months ago a similar brawl had found him incarcerated in a Police cell in Grantham the night his old crew went missing over Hamburg. His second tour on Lancasters now stretched over seven months and three Squadrons. Taffy had been among the best gunners on the Squadron at Waltham Grange; here at Ansham Wolds he was probably in a league of his own.

"Engineer to pilot," Ted Hallowes reported over the intercom. "Hatches closed and secure. OK to taxi, Skipper!"

Adam leaned out of the cockpit window and gestured for the ground crew to haul away the chocks. He saw an erk crawl beneath the scything, churning arc of the port-inner Merlin's propeller, watched as the man tugged and kicked at the wooden block half-buried and jammed under the great bulbous tyre. The tip of the propeller was spinning at 1,200 revs inches from the erk's face as he struggled with the chock. Another man edged under the Merlin's lethal blade. The chock was dragged clear.

The road was clear for B-Baker to roll.

There was a loud hiss of air as Adam released the brakes and the bomber jolted onto the perimeter road. Other Lancasters were starting up, but they had the road to themselves. He tried to keep off the brakes, manoeuvre the aircraft by juggling the revs solely on the outer Merlins.

He lined-up for takeoff.

"Auto-controls - clutch...IN."

"Cock...OUT."

"D.R. Compass...NORMAL."

"Pitot head heater switch...ON."

"Trimming tabs...ELEVATOR SLIGHTLY FORWARD - RUDDER NEUTRAL - AILERON IS NEUTRAL."

"Prop controls...FULLY UP."

"Fuel...MASTER ENGINE COCKS ARE ON - TANK SELECTOR COCKS SET TO NUMBER TWO TANKS - CROSS FEED COCK IS OFF - BOOSTER PUMPS IN NUMBERS ONE AND TWO TANKS ARE ON."

"Superchargers...MOD."

"Air intake...COLD."

"Rad shutter switches...AUTOMATIC."

"Flaps...FIFTEEN DEGREES DOWN."

Adam slid his right hand into position behind the throttles, eased the levers forward to zero boost against the brakes. The response was even, he throttled back. It was routine, second nature. The runway stretched away into the distance, the far end shrouded in a mist of falling rain.

"Clear to take-off, Skipper!" Ted Hallowes shouted in his ear. He leaned over his pilot's shoulder and placed his hand behind Adam's on the throttles.

"Lock throttles!"

"LOCKED!"

Adam flicked on his intercom. "Pilot to crew.

Prepare for take-off." One last deep breath, then: "Pilot to rear-gunner. Okay behind?"

"Rear gunner to Skipper. Okay behind!"

Adam pressed the throttles forward. When he reached zero boost he released the brakes. B-Baker picked up speed, fast. The acceleration pressed him gently back into his seat. As he opened the throttles he advanced those for the port Merlins slightly ahead of those for the starboard pair, offsetting the propeller torque which otherwise swung a Lancaster to the left as it gathered momentum. Unladen, the aircraft bounded down the runway. A touch on the brakes and the tail lifted off the wet tarmac as if the great monster was simply a four-engine Spitfire. All Lancaster pilots knew that God was on their side at moments like this...

Hallowes bellowed the increasing speeds. "Seventy...Seventy-five..."

Adam held the charging heavy arrow-straight down the centreline of the runway. "Full power!" He demanded, taking his hand off the throttles.

"Full power!" Hallowes repeated, pushing the throttles hard up against the stops. "Eighty... Eight-five... Ninety... Ninety-five... One hundred... And five... Ten..."

B-Baker flew.

With her fuel tanks mostly empty and no bombs in her cavernous bomb bay, B-Baker did not so much fly, as soar like an eagle. The shaking and buffeting stopped and the aircraft steadied in Adam's hands.

"Climbing power! Now!"

The Flight engineer pushed the throttles through the gate. B-Baker climbed high over the perimeter fence. Given her head the bomber would reach for the heavens with a grace and a hunger that would have taken a Halifax, Stirling or Wellington pilot's breath away. In this *light* condition Adam always felt as if he could out fly anything in the sky other than a well handled single-engine fighter. He had absolute confidence in the Merlins and the airframe.

The *Pilot's Notes* might caution: 'the aircraft is designed for manoeuvres appropriate to a heavy bomber and care must be taken to avoid imposing excessive loads with the elevators in recovery from dives and turns at high speed', but Adam took this with a pinch of salt. Likewise the warning that: 'spinning and aerobatics are not permitted' and that 'violent use of the rudder at high speeds should be avoided'. In moments of madness he used to wonder what would happen if he ever deliberately attempted to barrel roll a Lanc – in a *light* condition, obviously, rather than with a full bomb load onboard – but he had never actually tried it. He strongly suspected that given a safe altitude, somewhere around ten thousand feet ought to do the trick, rolling a Lancaster would be a breeze. Why not? In comparison to some of the manoeuvres he had lived through shaking off night fighters over Germany, a straightforward barrel roll, especially in daylight over England without the distraction of an attacking night fighter, would seem like a *breeze*. Well, as long as the wings did not come off...

"Wheels up."

Adam banked the Lancaster into a wide, climbing turn over the villages of Thurlby-le-Wold and Ansham Wolds, and circled back towards the airfield. In the west the River Trent rolled greyly north to where the Humber Estuary lay hidden in the murk. At two thousand feet B-Baker brushed the wispy satin lower edge of the overcast and he levelled off.

"Cruising power." The song of the Merlins quietened.

Adam scanned the sky. He had hoped to fly across country to the coast, make the flight a proper test of the new aircraft but there was no point taking unnecessary risks. Time enough for that tonight.

"Pilot to navigator."

"What can I do for you, Skipper?"

"Our jaunt to Spurn Head is off. Looks like the cloud base is descending. I'm going to do a couple of circuits and call it a day. Over."

"Navigator to pilot," Ben returned, feigning disappointment. "I only came along because you said we were going to the seaside."

Adam grinned, flicked the intercom switch.

"I wondered why you brought your bucket and spade!"

He pushed B-Baker's blunt nose around to the west into a long, slow turn over Lincolnshire. As the Lancaster wheeled the mottled coat of the wolds stretched away in every direction, a patchwork of interlinked hedgerows and fields, woods, uncultivated chalk downland, tracks and hamlets, isolated farms and barns. In the north the aerodrome lay like a fresh open wound upon the face of the land: the triangle of runways, the paler scars of the dispersals, the row of hangars, the Nissen-hutted barrack-town sharply defined against the grey-green and brown of the high wold.

"Pilot to crew. Keep your eyes peeled, chaps."

Ben had come up to the cockpit, braced himself against the back of Adam's seat, adding his eyes to those of the gunners. Patting the engineer's arm to signal that he had taken over his watching vigil his hard stare began to quarter the sky.

Ted Hallowes concentrated on his control board.

"Pilot to engineer. What do the dials say, Ted?"

"She's behaving herself like a real good 'un, Skipper!"

"Pilot to crew," Adam decided after two fifteen mile-wide circuits of the aerodrome. "I'm going to put down before the weather closes in. Everybody shut up while I call control." Even as he spoke B-Baker was enveloped in the cloud. He eased the bomber down until it emerged again into open skies. He switched channel and called up the ground controller. "B-Baker to

Chestnut control. Permission to land, over."

A woman's clipped, painstakingly precise voice came over the intercom.

"Hello B-Baker, this is Chestnut control. Pancake! Pancake! QFE one-zero-zero-seven, over."

"Roger, Chestnut control. QFE one-zero-zero-seven."

Adam checked the altimeter setting, corrected it to 1007 millibars. Zero on B-Baker's altimeter now corresponded to three hundred feet above sea level, the approximate elevation of Ansham Wolds. He juggled the throttles, reduced airspeed as Hallowes shouted out the landing drill.

"Auto-pilot control...OUT."

"Superchargers...IN M RATIO."

"Air intake...SET TO COLD."

"Brake pressure...SHOWING TWO-EIGHT-OH POUNDS."

Adam had lost count of how many times he had landed a Lancaster. His actions were governed by endless practice, habit deeply ingrained by ceaseless repetition. The first time he had got his hands on a Lanc he had flown it night and day, in all weathers, taking off and landing until everything became a natural reflex and nothing surprised him. He could land a Lanc blindfold.

"Flaps...TWENTY DEGREES - DOWN ANGLE."

"Undercarriage...DOWN AND NO WARNING LIGHT."

"Prop controls...UP AND REVS ARE OK."

"Fuel...BOOSTER PUMPS ARE ON IN NUMBER TWO TANKS."

B-Baker was on final approach, sinking down an invisible stairway towards the runway at one hundred and twenty knots of indicated airspeed, passing through four hundred feet.

All was well, everything was routine.

"CLIMB RIGHT!" The scream shattered the calm of the cockpit, sent a shiver of terror down the pilot's spine. "CLIMB RIGHT! GO! GO! GO!"

Adam reacted before the sound of the first horrified squeal of panic gave way to intercom static.

"Climbing power!" He yelled. B-Baker was at the point of no return. At the point of no return or very, very near to it, within a hair's breadth of being committed to landing. The abyss loomed before him and he glanced over the edge. Before him the road forked: one way ended in death, the other in life. The controls shook under his hands, death beckoned, its talons reaching up to drag him down into its dark, burning maw. He shoved the throttles hard through the stops. B-Baker's Merlins bellowed in agony as he dragged the Lancaster to starboard, battled to arrest her descent. He felt Ted Hallowes's hand roughly press against his, holding the throttles hard forward, he snatched his own hand away, hauled back on the controls with both arms. The great engines raged, clawed at the air, wrestling B-Baker away from the ground. The bomber shuddered from nose to tail, for a ghastly moment it balanced precariously on the knife edge of a stall. There she hung for one, two, three seconds that felt like an eternity. If B-Baker stalled there was no escape. She would fall out of the sky and they would die, quickly, fierily.

Then the moment passed, the terror ebbed.

B-Baker surged upward, riding the wave of horsepower generated by her brand new Merlins. With her fuel tanks three-quarters empty and no bomb load she was light, as fleet and nimble as any heavy bomber could be, and today, she was lucky, also.

Adam collected his wits. The warning had originated from the rear gunner.

"Taffy!" He demanded, bypassing normal intercom protocol. "What the bloody hell's going on?"

"There was another Lanc, Skipper," reported the gunner, shakily. His voice betrayed the fact that he, too, had just seen his life flash before his eyes. "Right alongside, it was. It never saw us. Flew in below us. We almost landed on top of it, Skipper. Jesus, I ain't never seen another Lanc that close to..."

Ben touched his pilot's shoulder. Adam followed his pointing arm back towards the airfield where a lone Lancaster was landing. He levelled off at a thousand feet, throttled back.

"Pilot to crew. Calm down everybody. Panic over."

Re-commencing the landing checklist he began to simultaneously plot the public hanging, drawing and quartering of the comedian who had flown unannounced, uninvited, unauthorized and certainly negligently into the circuit. It was one thing going for a burton on ops, another altogether buying it on a routine test flight through no fault of one's own. His appetite for summary vengeance was whetted further when it was discovered, upon landing that the other Lancaster had parked on B-Baker's hard stand.

A Bedford truck followed B-Baker half-way around the aerodrome as the bomber taxied to the next vacant dispersal. The Lancaster jolted to a halt and the worried members of the ground crew spilled over the rear tailgate of the lorry, scurrying to tend to their charge.

"She's all yours, Flight," Adam said gruffly to the flight-sergeant fitter in command of R-Robert's erks. "I didn't hear anything break, but get your chaps to have a damned good crawl over her, anyway. Every inch of her. Just to be on the safe side."

"Yes, sir!" The other man saluted smartly and bawled orders.

"Taffy!" Adam barked, his frown deepening. The diminutive Welshman came over to him, smiling smugly.

"Sir?"

"And you can stop 'sirring' me like that you scruffy little beggar!"

"Sorry, Skipper," the gunner muttered, smile fading. He had worked out he could probably get away with murder with the Wingco on his side; were it not for the fact it really did not pay to chance your arm with a CO like the Skipper. Besides, the Skipper was the one man in the RAF that Taffy Davies was actually a little – albeit just a little – afraid of.

"Not when you've just saved our bacon," Adam relented. "You saved all our lives back there." It was said quietly, sincerely. Airman to airman. "Thank you."

Taffy did not know how to deal with this. He bowed his head in embarrassment, shuffled his feet. The other members of the crew were straining to overhear what was going on, edging closer.

"Only doin' me job, Skipper."

"Nevertheless. It was a jolly good thing you were on the ball. How close was the other kite?"

"Didn't see how we could miss it. God's truth, Skipper. Didn't see how we could miss it until we did, like."

"Pretty close, then." At Adam's direction the Bedford transported the crew across the windswept infield directly to the watchtower. After their recent intimate brush with death nobody was feeling overly talkative. When they arrived Adam jumped down first and ran straight up the steps to the top of the tower where he saw that a crowd had gathered. Having kept the lid on his temper on the ride back the red mist now descended. With a vengeance. "Where's the so and so who was flying that Lanc?"

A firm hand took him by the elbow. "Steady on, old chap," pacified Group Captain Alexander, adopting his most paternal, fatherly tone.

Shaking off the Station Master's restraining arm Adam found himself blinking into the freckled face of a young woman in full flying sheepskins. She was peering at him from behind the relative safety of Barney Knight's broad shoulder, wearing the mildly vexed look of somebody who could not for the life of her work out what all the fuss was about.

"You?" He asked stupidly, the wind spilling from his sails. "You? You were flying that Lanc?"

"Actually, yes," she confessed, a little apologetically. Her accent was plummy, undoubtedly the honed product of an expensive finishing school. "I'm afraid I'm still getting the hang of things. I'm used to ferrying Spitfires and Hurricanes, you see. I've only just started doing Lancasters. Lancasters are a bit bigger and take a lot of getting used to. Although, now that I think about it, they aren't anywhere near as complicated to fly as the latest Halifaxes. Anyway, I was looking for Binbrook and I got a bit lost, what with this filthy old cloud everywhere. I thought this was Kirmington. When I called them up they said they couldn't see me but as there weren't any other aeroplanes in the circuit it was all right for me to come in and land." She laughed sweetly, gazed around the circle of faces. "You can imagine how silly I felt when Mr. Knight came out to meet me and told me this was Ansham Wolds. I'm most dreadfully sorry to be such a nuisance."

Nobody said a word. The woman rolled her eyes at Adam.

His hands trembled as he fumbled for his cigarette case. He did not find it, it was in his quarters. He never carried it on test flights. Somebody gave him a cigarette, and struck a match. He inhaled, sighed.

"Forgive me. I do apologise," he said, smiling his graveyard smile. "Please, forgive my shortness. It was unforgivable of me."

Belatedly, Ben arrived on the scene. He heard the laughter. Seeing the woman in the big, clumsy flying sheepskins he instantly put two and two together. Barney Knight caught the big man's eye, and winked mischievously.

"Three cheers for the gallant ladies of the ATS!" He called, grinning.

Ben joined in the 'hurrahs!' with a somewhat forced

enthusiasm.

Adam began to laugh. He laughed and laughed. Laughed until the tears rolled down his cheeks and his chest hurt. He stopped laughing only when Group Captain Alexander took him aside. The Old Man was wearing a stern face.

"Just to let you know. We're on for Hagen, tonight."

Chapter 2

Friday 1st October, 1943
The Gatekeeper's Lodge, Ansham Wolds, Lincolnshire

Eleanor moved about the kitchen softly humming the melody of an old song, something happy she had forgotten the words to long ago. Not even her encounter - outside the Rectory that afternoon - with that insufferable little man Edward Rowbotham, could dent her good humour. The ARP Warden had approached her to notify her that he had reported 'two further infringements of Parish blackout regulations' to the 'District ARP Committee', and that she would be informed as to her fate in 'due course'. The pompous little man! All he lacked was a stupid toothbrush moustache and he would be a perfect little Hitler! Apparently, she could now expect to be fined up to 'five pounds', and summoned before the local justices. The District ARP Committee, indeed! Half-a-dozen busybodies in reserved occupations! Not a real man among them!

'Calm down, Ellie,' she had told herself. 'They're not worth it!'

'Thank you, Mr Rowbotham,' she had smiled. 'I'm about to make a pot of tea for the Rector. Will you join us? I'm sure the Rector and his wife would be delighted to see you.'

'No, thank you,' the man had muttered stiffly, frowning uncomfortably as if she had just propositioned him in front of his wife and children. 'I have my official duties to attend to.'

Eleanor had looked him in the eye. 'Of course, with so many men away fighting somebody has to keep the home fires burning.' Ansham Wold's Chief ARP Warden had recoiled as if she had slapped his face, turned on his heel and stalked off in high dudgeon. 'What a rude little man,' she had murmured at his retreating back.

Thinking about it Eleanor giggled; she immediately silently admonished herself as she moved around the kitchen. If she was hauled up in front of a magistrate what sort of an example was she setting her children? If it came to it she would simply pay her fine and be done with it. She could not afford five pounds but she would find the money from somewhere, even if she had to stint herself, go without for a month or two. So long as she had food and warmth for her children, the last thing she was going to do was give *Mister* Rowbotham the satisfaction of besting her. Nor was she going to complain, least of all to her father. The cottage was warm and quiet, and the children were tucked up in their beds. Collecting the tea pot, milk, cups and saucers onto a tray she returned to the parlour where her father was reading by the fireside. On her return he put down his book.

"You look tired, my dear," he said, regarding her in that perspicacious way of his which she used to find so infuriating.

"You're imagining it," she returned, brightly.

The old man watched her settle in the chair opposite him and busy herself pouring the tea. Eleanor reminded him so much of her dear departed mother. So much so that sometimes the very sight of her prompted an irreconcilable ache deep within him. She had her mother's silent strength, the self-same Sephardic stillness in her eyes, the same dark, arresting inner beauty.

"You really mustn't worry about me," Eleanor chided him. "I'm all right. Really I am." Wood burned, sap crackled in the flames. She sipped her tea, wrapped herself in the blanket of her thoughts. Although her father would not admit it he was growing visibly frailer. Since his illness in the spring they had grown very close. Closer perhaps, than they had ever been. When she was young he was always a stranger, a kind, quirky, lovable stranger but for all that, a stranger. Then, when she had married they had nearly lost touch, they had become oddly estranged and only latterly, drawn close again. Without saying a word, without raking over the coals, they had set aside their differences, and become reconciled. "It's cold for this time of year. Don't you think?"

"Yes, a little."

"Shall we have snow this winter, do you think?" Eleanor asked, staring distractedly into the fire. "The children would like snow."

"I'm not sure the RAF would share the children's' sentiments, my dear," her father decided, not without irony.

"No, I suppose not."

Her father laughed his patient laugh. It broke into Eleanor's spell and she looked up from the fire.

"Whatever is it?"

"Nothing. Simply an old man's perversity of mind."

"Oh."

He sat up in the armchair, reached across and patted her knee.

"Here we are, you and I, sitting in the middle of Bomber Command Country," he declared, not troubling to conceal his fond amusement. "Sitting at the very heart of a great crusade that someday will be the bane of generations of historians. They won't begin to understand what's going on around us now. Not one bit of it. But make no mistake, here in dear old Ansham Wolds we are surrounded by men who are shaping the course of this war, and probably the course of human history for goodness knows how many years to come. And yet," he paused, whimsically, "from a child's point of view the only thing that matters is for there to be snow this winter."

Eleanor gave him a quizzical look.

"That's all very well," she retorted. Her father sometimes talked the most awful nonsense. "Surely, that only goes to show that children have a great deal more sense than the so-called grown-ups in this world!" She had no patience for anybody who tried to conceal the ghastliness of the war in a pretty basket of words. The war had already taken her children's father, a kind, sweet man, from her and not a day went by without her thinking about her boisterous, fun-loving baby brother rotting in some unspeakable Prussian prison camp. So far as she was concerned the sooner the whole dreadful business was finished the better.

"I don't suppose you have much contact with the aerodrome?" Her father inquired, out of the blue.

"Only indirectly. Occasionally."

The old man detected her defensiveness, latched onto it.

"Occasionally?"

Eleanor's brow furrowed. "I met David's old CO."

"Chantrey? Adam Chantrey?"

"He was waiting for the train before yours. He was meeting his Navigation Leader, Squadron Leader Hardiman. He was on the earlier train. It was funny," she went on, her thoughts twirling around the brief encounter, "I expected him to be older..."

"I thought Bert Fulshawe was in charge up the road?"

The woman shook her head.

"No, not any more. They say he was killed in a crash last week."

"Oh, I'm sorry to hear that. Wizard chap. I am sorry. Poor Bert."

"I didn't realise you knew Wing-Commander Fulshawe," Eleanor apologised, beginning to regret that she had mentioned her chance meeting with the dead man's successor.

"I didn't. Not really. Only by reputation. Bumped

into him once or twice, that sort of thing," her father replied quickly. Rather too quickly. "So, they've installed Adam Chantrey at Ansham Wolds, have they? Last time I had any dealings with him he was CO at Waltham Grange. Before that he was on the Chief's staff at High Wycombe. Or was he off night fighting? Or was that before he was on the Chief's staff? I forget. No, he was on Blenheim night fighters before he went to Boscombe Down and before he took over 380 Squadron at Kelmington last year. *Then*, he was on the Chief's personal staff at Bomber Command HQ at High Wycombe. My, my, the boy certainly gets around, what?"

"Oh," Eleanor breathed, her demeanour a study in polite indifference. Privately, her curiosity churned. Her father rarely spoke about his work at the Air Ministry. What he did remained a mystery to her, a tightly closed book. She hardly knew what to make of this sudden talkativeness.

"Chantrey got his first DFC on one of those early daylight shows to Heligoland or somewhere around there. Wilhelmshaven rings a bell. Yes, it could have been the Wilhelmshaven do. His first op, I think. Anyway, his aircraft got hit – navigator and one of the gunners were killed and Bert Fulshawe was out for the count - and he brought the plane back on one engine. Put it down on the beach at Southwold. He got another DFC on night fighters, I think. Did you know David was with him on the Le Creusot show, by the way? Into France, detouring around Paris at low-level in broad daylight!" The old man shook his grey head, chuckled softly. "They say the only way the Chief could get him to stop flying ops was to post him to High Wycombe so he could personally keep his eye on him!"

Eleanor tried to stop herself but a question popped out.

"The Chief?"

Again, her father laughed. "Forgive me, my dear. The Chief is He whom we mere mortals know as Air Chief-Marshall Sir Arthur Travers Harris, Air Officer Commanding-in-Chief, Bomber Command."

She registered both the irony and the grudging respect in his voice. Her brother had crowed over the things 'Bomber' Harris had promised he was going to do to the Jerries. Of course, David had gone to war in aircrew blue, not Whitehall grey. She brought herself up short, instantly. That was unfair. Her father had commanded a rifle company in Flanders in the Great War, led his men over the top, been wounded more than once, before eventually being invalided home. In his own way he was every inch as much a fighting man as her brother. The difference was that David had always looked the part. With his cap tipped up over one eye, the faded wings on his battledress, the swagger in his walk and a twinkle in his eye her brother had loved every minute of his war. Probably right up to the moment he was shot down. How he must hate to be caged, excluded from all the fun. Poor Dave.

It was later when Eleanor was clearing away the cups and saucers that she heard the unmistakable sound of Merlin engines starting up. The distant thunder of countless engines soon rolled across the high wold, battered against her kitchen windows and assailed her ears.

"I wonder where they're off to tonight?" Her father thought out aloud, standing in the doorway.

Eleanor was thinking about Adam Chantrey.

He would be flying tonight.

The first Lancaster into the air would be his.

Chapter 3

Friday 1st October, 1943
Lancaster B-Baker, 90 miles East of Cromer

The Lancaster Force was going to war, flooding into the east, an irresistible tsunami sweeping towards the small industrial town of Hagen, twelve miles south of Dortmund.

Climbing hard B-Baker emerged from the clouds thirteen thousand feet above the North Sea into a clear starry autumn night. The bomber handled leadenly, sulkily for all the massive, pulsing power of her straining Merlin XXs. She was talking to Adam through the controls, telling him she did not want to climb another inch. He made her climb, anyway.

That afternoon he had personally supervised the nailing of a new sign over the entrance to the Officers' Mess:

H-E-I-G-H-T SPELLS S-A-F-E-T-Y

It was the oldest home truth, so Adam drove B-Baker higher and higher. The Lancaster Manual for the Marks I and III - the Merlin-engine variants which now equipped virtually all the operational squadrons of Nos 1 and 5 Groups - cautioned that 'flying should be restricted to straight and level until weight has been reduced to 63,000 pounds'. Tonight, at his instigation, each of 647 Squadron's Lancasters had taken off more than a ton over-weight. It was necessary. The Squadron had a point to prove and its good name to recover. He had promised that things would change and tonight was as good a time as any to commence that change. Words counted for only so much. Deeds spoke louder than any words.

"Gentlemen, in future 647 Squadron will fly ops at a maximum all-up weight of sixty-five thousand pounds," Adam had announced at the main crew briefing, reducing the crews to a state of numbed, disbelieving incredulity. "Tonight this will enable each aircraft to carry an additional twelve hundred pounds of incendiaries, and another seventy gallons of fuel. The extra fuel will compensate for any increase in consumption rates due to the increase in take-off weights." The hall had been half-empty, a painful reminder that the Squadron was operating at what was, effectively, half-strength. "I will be flying B-Baker tonight. B-Baker will be the first aircraft to take-off and B-Baker will be carrying the same bomb load as your aircraft. However, B-Baker will also be carrying two additional five hundred pound general purpose bombs. For luck!"

Adam did not normally believe in 'gestures'. Or, for that matter, in taking undue risks. However, this was his first and best chance of grabbing the Squadron by the scruff of the neck. The crews needed a good night. Something they could be proud of, something to boast about in the Mess, a reason to hold their heads high; and by hook or by crook, he was going to give them one. Besides, increasing the takeoff weights of his Lancasters was the most meticulously calculated of risks.

Getting airborne had been relatively straightforward. He had held the Lancaster down as long as possible with the throttles at maximum boost, eased back on the controls at the end of the runway and B-Baker had lifted smoothly off the tarmac. Climbing was the problem. The operations plan specified the enemy coast should be crossed at an altitude of 20,000 feet. B-Baker was unlikely to achieve this height until forty to fifty miles inside enemy territory.

"Fuel consumption?" Adam rasped into the intercom.

"Over the odds, Skipper," Ted Hallowes replied, evenly. "But nothing to worry about." As B-Baker's Merlins drank fuel, her weight would decrease and she would eventually become again, the vibrant, obedient creature that she had been that afternoon.

"Navigator to pilot," Ben called. "Enemy coast ahead. Eight minutes. Expect some flak. Nothing serious."

"Pilot to crew," Adam drawled, laconically. "Wake up everybody. Bandit country up ahead. Out."

Ben listened to his friend's dry, matter of fact delivery, smiled and shook his head. Behind the blackout curtain that separated him from the engineer and the pilot the ghostly loom of the *H2S* cathode ray tube display lit his face. At the top of the small, flickering screen was the jittering, fuzzy white outline of the Dutch coast.

In the old days a device like *H2S* would have been unthinkable, pure black magic. Nowadays, the navigation fraternity could call upon flawed magic embodied in not one, but two, electronic aids. *H2S* and the *TR1335* set, codenamed *Gee*. Of the two *H2S* was the newer and moodier beast – as yet available to only a few aircraft per Main Force squadron - while *Gee* was a comparatively domesticated animal.

Gee had been standard equipment on Bomber Command's heavies for eighteen months. The set received transmissions from ground stations in England and used them to establish – by simple triangulation - the aircraft's approximate position up to a range of between two and three hundred miles from base, depending on the altitude at which the aircraft was flying and the prevailing atmospheric conditions. Exceptionally, Ben had once picked up *Gee* transmissions over the Alps on a trip to Milan. Since then the Germans had begun to jam it, restricting the device's reach to the north-western shores of Europe, rendering it useless on deep penetrations into Germany. Notwithstanding *Gee's* declining usefulness over enemy territory, over England, night after night it safely guided the Main Force home.

H2S equipped all Pathfinder aircraft. The device was a downward-pointing microwave radar housed in a large, bulbous cupola slung below the aft fuselage between the mid-upper turret and the tail plane. Theoretically, it presented navigators with a radar 'picture' of the terrain over which the bomber was flying. Black magic, indeed! There were plans afoot to equip every Main Force Lancaster and Halifax with *H2S* in the coming months but presently, B-Baker was one of only three *H2S*-equipped 647 Squadron Lancasters. Unfortunately, *H2S* was far from being the finished article. The boffins were working on a new three-centimetre wavelength set which might eventually produce better results but for all Ben knew, that was a pipe-dream. For the present he was stuck with the existing ten-centimetre set which often gave contradictory, if not wholly mystifying reflections of the topography below. Over a sprawling urban landscape such as that of a large industrial city, the screen became a white haze of ground returns. Worse than useless. Even in the hands of a skilled operator, other than over water, rivers, estuaries or coastlines it was a liability, a positive menace. To many, the device's codename, *H2S*, was apt: like bad eggs, it stank. Moreover, the set had an evil habit of bursting into flames. This was not good news on aircraft routinely packed with ten tons of 100-octane fuel, high explosives and incendiaries!

Ben switched off *H2S* as B-Baker crossed the Dutch coast. Having used the set to confirm the bomber's landfall, barring emergencies he would not turn the set on again until they were running for home over northern France. Since *H2S* functioned by transmitting radio waves, theoretically, any fighter equipped with a suitable receiver could home in on its signals. The intelligence clan had closed ranks, declared that there was not a single shred of evidence that the Luftwaffe had 'worked out' *H2S*, yet. 'Yet' being the operative clause. Old lags like Ben Hardiman had learned the hard way that the Germans tended to work most things out sooner rather than later.

Better safe than sorry.

The *H2S* screen went dark.

Tonight, Ben would rely on dead-reckoning and star sights to get them to the target in the certain knowledge that once over the target, a third piece of electronic wizardry mounted in high flying twin-engine 8 Group Mosquitoes would do the rest: *Oboe*.

Oboe was the blind-bombing system Bomber Command had employed to raze the cities of the Ruhr and the Rhineland that spring and summer. By some unaccountable oversight - perhaps some chinless wonder at Command had mislaid the town's target file - Hagen had been neglected during the course of that earlier campaign. Tonight, the Main Force had been warned that the target was likely to be under ten-tenths cloud. A year ago this might have saved Hagen. A year ago the Main Force might have scattered its bombs across the Ruhr Valley and the town might have come through completely unscathed, and lived to fight another day.

Tonight, *Oboe* would be the death of Hagen.

Oboe was simple both in concept and operation. Ground stations in England transmitted two beams, so called 'cat' and 'mouse' signals. High-flying Pathfinder Mosquitoes flew along one 'ranging' beam - usually at over thirty thousand feet - until they crossed the second 'directional' beam, at which point they dropped Sky Markers for the Main Force to bomb. The range at which the system operated was limited only by the curvature of the earth. While the cities of central, eastern and southern Germany were currently beyond its deadly reach, safe from *Oboe's* intersecting *cat* and *mouse* transmissions, it was Hagen's tragedy that it lay well within *Oboe's* killing zone.

"Flak in front!" Called Round Again from his position in the nose.

Ben Hardiman grinned under his oxygen mask as he heard Adam Chantrey's terse acknowledgment lance through the hissing static.

"Pilot to bomb-aimer. No need to get excited, Angus. Bearing and range, please!"

Chastened, the bomb-aimer reported that the flak was ten degrees to port and approximately five miles distant.

Ben left his desk and his maps to see for himself. He stood behind the pilot's seat for about a minute. The flak was sparse, a bit apologetic. Nevertheless, all flak was worth noting for future reference. He stretched briefly, stamped his feet against the inroads of the cold and returned to his cluttered cubby-hole, inadvertently catching his right elbow on the sharp outcrop of the H2S screen's casing. He cursed vociferously over the open intercom channel.

"Something I said, old man?" Adam inquired, chuckling.

The intercom fell silent.

Adam held B-Baker on course, climbing, climbing. The Lancaster shouldered into the slipstream of an unseen heavy up ahead, welcome confirmation that although they had not seen another aircraft since take-off, they were not alone in the darkness of the night. The head of the bomber stream was pouring across the German border now. The fighter masters would be scrambling their squadrons, air raid sirens would be sounding all across north western Germany, the populations of whole cities would be scurrying down to the shelters. Countless eyes would soon turn to the heavens, anxiously awaiting the dazzling blaze of iridescence of the first Sky Markers, signalling the start of a nightmare.

"Pilot to bomb-aimer. Check your equipment. Then get weaving on the Windowing front."

"Roger, Skipper."

Window was the secret weapon that had granted Bomber Command licence to destroy Hamburg virtually unopposed in late July. *Window* was no more or less than strips of paper metalled on one side. Dropped in thousands by every aircraft in the bomber stream, the Germans called *Window* 'snow' because on some nights it produced an impenetrable 'white-out' effect on the screens of their long-range air search radars. It was the advent of Window that had forced the Germans to abandon their old night fighting tactics.

Over the years the defenders had painstakingly built up a sophisticated night fighter control and command system around the *Zahme Sau*, or *Tame Boar* tactic. Under this system the Germans divided the sky into boxes – initially three lines of overlapping boxes from the French coast to the German border, later progressively more lines deeper and deeper into Germany - and allocated each fighter a box within which it was vectored onto individual bombers as they flew through it. This defensive system, known as the *Kammhuber Line*, named for its creator Colonel Josef Kammhuber, had been designed in July 1940 to counter the apparently scatter gun tactics of Bomber Command. In those anarchic days of 1940 and 1941 aircraft had chosen their own routes to the target, and Squadrons selected their own takeoff and bombing times. *Zahme Sau* had been a pragmatic solution to the problem of how to pick off an enemy who contrary to the normal principles of war, rarely, if ever, concentrated his forces in either time or space. In 1942, once Bomber Command had acquired new navigational aids and learned the hard lessons the

Luftwaffe had taken for granted two years before, had, equally pragmatically, developed the tactic of the 'bomber stream' to overwhelm the *Kammhuber Line*; essentially, by flooding a small number of 'boxes' with the maximum number of heavies in the shortest possible time. By saturating the *Kammhuber Line* with scores, and latterly, hundreds of targets the Luftwaffe was never able to concentrate more than a relatively small fraction of its available night fighters against the bomber force at any one time. The defenders had become so wedded to Tame Boar that even after the introduction of bomber stream tactics, and in the face of a massively escalating bombing offensive they had doggedly persisted with it throughout 1942 and the first seven months of 1943.

It was only with the introduction of *Window* at the end of July 1943 that the Germans finally abandoned *Zahme Sau* because overnight, *Window* blinded the long-range *Freya* radars upon which *Zahme Sau* depended. *Window* was no more or less than strips of paper, metalized on one side, which, showered in sufficiently vast quantities by every aircraft in the bomber stream, *snowed*, or in English, 'jammed' the defenders' previously all-seeing interlocked network of *Freya* ground-based radar systems.

Briefly, *Window* had given Bomber Command licence to fire-raze virtually unopposed over Germany. Tens of thousands had been consumed in the Hamburg firestorm and later in August the Main Force had successfully attacked the Luftwaffe Experimental Establishment at Peenemunde.

Of course, in the nature of things the Luftwaffe had reacted swiftly to the introduction of *Window*. Once the enemy recovered from his initial shock, he had resorted to *Wilde Sau*, or *Wild Boar* tactics. Unlike *Tame Boar*, *Wild Boar* did not rely on precise, long-range detection and tracking. *Wild Boar* simply required the controllers to provide the *whole* night fighter force with a running commentary on the general position, speed and ground track of the bomber stream. Henceforth, it would be up to individual pilots to make contact with and then hunt alone - visually, or using their short-range onboard Liechtenstein radars which were less severely affected by Window - inside the bomber stream. On some nights recently, casualties had returned to pre-*Window*, pre-Hamburg levels.

On Lancasters, the task of '*Windowing*', physically shoving handfuls of *Window* down a chute in the freezing waist of the bomber usually fell to wireless operators. However, Adam preferred Bert Pound to play the frequencies, listen in on the night fighter traffic.

Besides, *Windowing* stopped Round Again getting over excited.

Chapter 4

Saturday 2nd October, 1943
RAF Ansham Wolds, Lincolnshire

Suzy drove Group Captain Alexander out to see off his heavies and then waited by the car within earshot of her passenger but as always on these occasions at a respectful distance.

The Old Man chatted amiably with the Squadron's senior officers while Lancasters revved their Merlins and rushed down the runway. The night was cool, clear and dry, and the flare path lights gave the onlookers an excellent view of the bombers as they hurtled into the distance, lifting gracefully into the air. Overhead, the sonorous, rumbling thunder of countless aircraft clawing for height over Lincolnshire tumbled down to earth like a sign from the gods.

"Where was it to be tonight?" Suzy asked herself.

Somewhere distant. She knew that much, at least. Maximum fuel and a reduced bomb load always meant somewhere distant. Somewhere distant and probably very, very dangerous. The news had got around and swelled the crowd of well-wishers. Tonight's crowd was the largest and loudest Suzy could ever recall.

The Group Captain was in a huddle with the new Wingco and the commander of A Flight, who had just been promoted to Acting Squadron Leader. Mr McDonald seemed a good sort, very quiet and thoughtful, polite, and punctiliously correct with every WAAF with whom he dealt. Not at all like Squadron Leader Knight. While the other girls agreed that Knight was as dishy as they came, nobody really liked him. He was rude, arrogant, quick to find fault, and too liable to fly off the handle without warning. He was also a dreadful flirt. In the Waafery they claimed no woman was safe in his company.

Last night the Squadron had sent 8 aircraft to Hagen in the Ruhr. Everybody had got back safely and the air of gloom and despondency which had settled over Ansham Wolds in recent weeks had lifted a little. Tonight, it was the turn of the crews who had missed out on the Hagen show.

The Wingco said something to Group Captain Alexander who laughed heartily. The new Wing-Commander was a strange one. Nothing ruffled him, nothing surprised him. He was a perfect gentleman and he and the Station Master seemed to have hit it off, immediately. Out of the corner of her eye Suzy saw the Wingco's dog ambling towards her.

"Hello, Rufus," she murmured and he allowed her to fuss over him. If Chantrey's predecessor, Wing-Commander Fulshawe, had had a dog it would have been a bulldog, a true-bred British bulldog, pugnacious and tenacious like his master. Rufus was a friendly, placid animal. A Mess dog. In the Mess they placed a half-a-pint jug of stout on the floor whenever he was in the vicinity. Suzy bent down, patted and stroked the dog's flank.

"I think you've made a conquest."

Suzy turned, looked up and in the glow of the flare path lights recognized the battered, smiling face of Flight-Lieutenant Tilliard. Their paths had not crossed since their meeting in the hospital, but several times she had glimpsed him from afar, limping, usually alone, lost in thought.

"Sorry," he said, quickly. "I didn't mean to startle you."

"No, it's all right. You didn't."

In the background L-London trundled to a halt at the threshold. The pitch of her engines rose as the pilot ran up his Merlins at zero boost against the brakes and fell as he throttled back.

"How are you, sir?"

Tilliard flinched at the 'sir'. It seemed misplaced. He felt guilty, in the wrong. Having more than once tried to engineer a chance encounter with ACW Mills, now that the meeting had actually materialised, like a fool he hardly knew what to say or do.

"A bit sore but otherwise up and about," he muttered, feebly. "As you see."

"That's good."

"I haven't had a chance to thank you properly for your visit the other day."

"Oh, that's all right," Suzy returned, lowering her eyes.

"No, really," he insisted. "I was feeling pretty low and you cheered me up no end."

The woman felt the heat rise in her cheeks and she glanced uncomfortably in the direction of the Squadron's senior officers who were locked in a jocular, animated discussion nearby. L-London was rolling, Merlins racing. The crowd vented a ragged cheer, waved her off into the night.

"They won't let me back in the air for at least another week or so," the man confided, attempting to laugh aside his angst and failing dismally.

"You took an awful knock, you know," she sympathised.

Tilliard had turned in on himself, suddenly aware of the awkwardness of the situation. This was a conversation that - according to King's Regulations - was not supposed to occur. He was deep in the forbidden territory of fraternization, tip-toeing through a minefield. The regulations were nothing if not explicit. Officers were officers; other ranks were other ranks. Officers and other ranks did not fraternize. Especially, if they were of different sexes. The fact that it went on all the time was incidental, no defence, and wholly inadmissible at a chap's court-martial.

"Oh, dear." He stared past the woman at L-London

charging down the runway bound for southern Germany. "I'm not very good at these things," he confessed, making a hash of trying to effect nonchalance. "Would it be all right if I was to ask you to take in a film with me? In Scunthorpe one night?"

Suzy's heart missed a beat. A thrill of excitement ran through her. She knelt down by Rufus, stroked his ears, patted him gently. She did not look up.

After a pause that seemed to last forever she murmured: "That would be lovely."

"Ah, Tilliard!" Boomed Group Captain Alexander. "Where have you been hiding?"

The pilot froze.

"We've just been talking about you!"

"Oh, really, sir?"

"Yes, don't stand on ceremony! Come on over and join the council of war." The Station Master's voice was full of a bonhomie that until now had been wholly, not to say conspicuously, absent in Tilliard's encounters with him. While the Old Man had treated him with robust courtesy, it had always been of the forthright kind reserved for, and understood by junior officers. Dutifully, Tilliard limped painfully towards Alexander.

"Up and about again, then, Peter," the Wingco grinned.

"Yes, sir. On the mend, thanks."

"Good. I want you to take over our new Conversion Flight. I want our sprogs flying until they drop. Mac's got quite enough on his plate without having to nurse maid our sprogs. He'll give you the lowdown. Any questions?"

"Er, no, sir," Tilliard stammered, stunned by this bombshell. "It was just that I was rather hoping to get back onto ops as soon as possible."

The loom of the flare path lights fell on their faces.

The Wingco looked Tilliard in the eye.

"You'll be back on ops as soon as the Flight Surgeon

gives you the green light, Peter. In the meantime, I'm not having an old lag like you twiddling his thumbs on terra firma when there's work to be done in the air."

Tilliard took this onboard. Earlier that day he had complained to Mac about his enforced inactivity. His friend had chuckled, intimated that the Wingco had plans for him and left him on tenterhooks. Once again he was struck by the contrast between Chantrey and Fulshawe. There was much of Bert Fulshawe's approach both in Chantrey's handling of briefings and in his dealings with groups of men; but man to man there was no artifice, no nonsense. The new Wingco looked you in the eye, calmly told you what you were going to do and why you were going to do it. A man knew exactly where he stood with him. With Bert Fulshawe – particularly at the end - you tended to drift in and out of favour at the drop of a hat, without warning, without reason.

"Don't panic, Peter," the Wingco smiled. "You'll be back on ops soon enough. But first you're going to get yourself fighting fit and you're going to knock *my* sprogs into shape for me. Okay?"

"Yes, sir."

The last Lancaster away was S-Sugar at 20:07 hours. Ansham Wolds had despatched nine aircraft in twenty-three minutes.

"Sloppy, gentlemen," the Wingco remarked, looking at his watch. "Plenty of room for improvement, what!" It was said almost conversationally but nobody was deceived. Although histrionics might not be the new Wingco's stock in trade, everybody listened when he spoke. Listened and took note. The Squadron's heavies ought to have been safely away in less than fifteen minutes. A minute to a minute-and-a-half or less between take offs was par for the course on the best Squadrons.

The crowd began to disperse.

Having hitched a lift out to the field on a passing

Bedford truck, Tilliard now faced a long, halting walk across the darkened aerodrome to return to the Mess. ACW Mills, whose first name he had still not discovered, had driven off with the Old Man.

"You absolute clot," he told himself. "Why on earth didn't you ask her name?"

He began to trudge down the road. Knots of well-wishers strolled past, chattering in the night like party-goers wending their way home.

Out of the night the Wingco's old Bentley growled to a halt beside him.

"Want a lift, Peter?"

"That's awfully decent of you, sir."

"You'll have to put up with Rufus on your lap, I'm afraid!"

The Alsatian obediently jumped out of the car, waited for the invalid to settle beside the driver and popped back in, dumping himself heavily, crushingly on Tilliard's lap. Rufus knew the drill. He was, notwithstanding his predilection for stout, a very well-trained dog.

"You all right there, old man?" Chantrey inquired, kicking the car into gear and rolling on into the night. Rufus stuck his snout into Tilliard's face, licked his cheek.

"Fine. Thank you, sir," he replied, pushing the dog's head aside.

"Have you made any progress putting together a crew?"

"Not a lot, sir. What with being laid up, I'm afraid."

"Oh, well. No immediate rush, what."

Chapter 5

Sunday 3rd October, 1943
Lancaster Z-Zebra, 8 miles NNE of Enkhuisen

Adam held Z-Zebra on course, climbing high above the invisible Zuider Zee three miles below. He eyed the flak up ahead with weary indifference. Standing orders required him to fly straight and level through flak. Pilots being human and burdened with human frailties tended to please themselves. The flak peppering the sky in the near distance looked blind, a single battery tossing up shells for the sake of it. Gunnery more in hope than expectation. Shortly after Z-Zebra flew through the fireworks Taffy Davies reported the guns had ceased firing.

"Rear gunner to pilot. The flak's just gone out, Skipper. Like a light!"

Adam drew the obvious inference. There were night fighters in the vicinity and the German area controller had ordered the local flak units to stand down.

"Pilot to gunners. Keep your eyes peeled for bandits." His playful tone belied his inner qualms. It was vital to keep things on an even keel, as businesslike as possible. "Looks like we may be having company soon. The bad guys are on their way up to meet us."

All the Squadron's aircraft had returned safely from Munich that morning. The last two trips had been exactly what the doctor ordered, with the Luftwaffe failing to significantly inconvenience the Main Force on either night. Unopposed, the Lancaster Force had made hay. Hagen, it seemed, had been particularly hard hit. According to Pat Farlane, most of the town no longer existed.

Z-Zebra droned on.

Tonight, a mixed Main Force of over 500 Lancasters, Halifaxes and Stirlings was bound for Kassel, a sprawling industrial city on the banks of the River Fulda. Situated far beyond the Ruhr, Kassel lay in the heart of Germany, mid-way between Hanover and Frankfurt-am-Main. The city had been attacked many times but to date Bomber Command had done it little lasting harm.

The coast was behind them now, the ground obscured by the leading edge of a weather front which extended across northern Europe from Belgium to the Baltic.

"Rear-gunner to pilot. Flamer astern at nine o'clock. Three, maybe four miles."

Adam swallowed. The fighters were already in the bomber stream. It was disconcertingly early in the proceedings for the first appearance of the hunters. He flicked his intercom switch.

"Must be the boys from Deelen and St. Trond," he remarked, evenly.

Fighters in the bomber stream at such an early stage in an op often signalled a long night's killing with the hunters harrying the Main Force all the way to the target. Flak could be a nightmarish thing; it was fighters that terrified the old lags. Flak was random, anonymous. Flak was something you could see and something you could come to terms with. A brush with a fighter was something else, personal, airman against airman with the odds stacked against the bomber. Fighters were strange, deadly creatures aircrew rarely encountered. Many men completed an entire tour of operations without ever laying eyes on a night fighter. Or more correctly, they completed a tour of ops precisely because they had never laid eyes on a fighter. Flak was dazzling, frightening stuff but much less likely to claim life and limb; fighters hacked down heavies in droves every time the Main Force struck at the distant cities. Having been both gamekeeper and poacher, Adam had no illusions. Once discovered, a lumbering heavy had little chance of escaping a well-handled night fighter.

Bomber crews in general and sprogs in particular, under-rated night fighters.

'Fighters!' They would crow, pint jug in hand in the Mess, winking knowingly. 'Fighters? Oh, we shoot them down, old boy! Bang! Bang! Bang!'

The trouble with a night fighter was that it was virtually invisible. Even if you did see it before it opened fire it was usually too late to do much about it. Night fighters lurked in the darkness of the night, prowled along the fringes of the bomber stream singling out victims. Like wolves descending upon the fold... A fighter was lost in the enormity and the blackness of the sky right up to moment it announced its presence with a burst of cannon fire. For countless Bomber Command aircrew their last moments on earth were filled with the chaos of tracer flashing in the night, the crash of cannon shells coming inboard, the screams of the maimed and the dying, and the fire and flames of Hades as their aircraft fell out of the sky.

Adam levelled Z-Zebra at twenty-one thousand feet crossing into Germany. He began to weave the bomber from one beam to the other, drunkenly, erratically. Pilots who flew straight and level when there were fighters about got letters posted to their next-of-kin, deservedly so. The Lancaster shuddered periodically as she bumped into the eddying propeller wash of another unseen heavy up ahead. The turbulence confirmed Z-Zebra was tucked into the body of the bomber stream. This knowledge was always a comfort for stragglers were meat and drink to the hunters.

Twin tracers tracked across the sky, distantly. Immediately, there was a flicker of fire. Five seconds later a heavy detonated, spreading a brief, crimson ball about itself. It fell in half-a-dozen burning pieces, tumbling, tumbling down.

Yes, like wolves upon the fold...

"Heavy going down at four o'clock," Round Again

called out from the nose. "Range five miles. Night fighter, maybe."

"Pilot to navigator," Adam added, tersely. "Confirm that as a fighter kill. I saw tracer fire before the kite exploded. There was no flak."

Ben Hardiman acknowledged the reports and noted them on his pad. There were many crews who steadfastly refused to recognise exploding heavies for what they were. They described them in their logs as 'scarecrows'. 'Scarecrow' theorists claimed the enemy was firing special shells into the bomber stream to mimic the appearance of bombers blowing up in mid air.

'Psychological warfare, and all that?' He had queried when he had first heard this claptrap spouted in earnest.

'That's right.'

Neither Ben, nor his pilot believed in *scarecrow shells*. There was no such shell. Common sense told them that there was only one thing looked like a heavy, its cookie and several tons of 100-octane fuel igniting in mid-air; a bomber blowing up. The Germans had no need to manufacture *scarecrow shells* when so many heavies blew up, anyway.

By now a gamut of diversionary operations would be coming to fruition: a small force of Stirlings was *gardening* - sowing sea mines - off the Frisian Islands; ten Pathfinder Mosquitoes, *Windowing* frantically, were mounting a spoof raid on Hanover; a dozen Mosquitoes were carrying out an *Oboe*-controlled attack on the Knapsack power station complex near Cologne; others were off to Aachen; Fighter Command intruders were operating over France and the low countries; and OTU crews were busily laying false *Window* trails over the North Sea. Nothing out of the ordinary. Nothing likely to divert the enemy's attention overlong from the Main Force as it penetrated deeper and deeper into Germany.

"Rear gunner to pilot. Flamer going down astern at seven o'clock. Range five miles. Didn't see any tracer but there was no flak."

Adam carried on weaving Z-Zebra.

They were still at least an hour's flying time from Kassel.

And the wolves were upon the fold...

Chapter 6

Monday 4th October, 1943
Ansham Wolds, Lincolnshire

The village of Ansham Wolds straggled along the contours of the valley. On either side farmland dominated the landscape while in the south an ancient stone church, St Paul's, stood atop a low hill overlooking its parish. The ivy-clad rectory sat squarely on the hillside beneath the churchyard, and beyond it nestling in the trees, was the ugly wooden church hall. The Ansham Wolds Memorial Church Hall – erected to commemorate the district's fallen from the Great War in 1921 - had served as the village's only school for over two decades. Beyond it the woods fell back around the hillside, and climbed the High Wold all the way up to the boundary fence of the aerodrome.

The woods and most of the land on which the airfield was built had, until a few years before the war formed part of an estate passed down through eight generations of the Grafton family before the Depression finally bankrupted the dynasty. At its heart, Ansham Hall, the once proud ancestral seat of the Grafton's, now lay like the family's fortunes, in irredeemable ruin.

Twenty years ago Eleanor would have been the lady of the manor. Not that she had ever wasted her time contemplating what might have been. She was content to rent the Gatekeeper's Lodge. It was a picturesque old cottage, well-founded, warm and quiet, sheltered by overhanging oaks and elms with its own small, walled garden. The Lodge had no mains water or electricity, water had to be pumped by hand from the well in the garden and lighting was by oil lamps and candles. Nevertheless, Eleanor did not miss the comforts of city life. There was kindling aplenty for the kitchen range, and to keep the fire in the parlour blazing; much to be said for the joys of the simple life. It was no hardship to draw water from the well, or light candles in the evening, or in having to walk into the village to make a telephone call and if the joys of having to use an outside privy were few and far between in the depths of winter, it was one cross she and the children simply had to bear.

Most mornings she walked her children through the trees past the derelict shell of Ansham Hall and through the overgrown landscape gardens, around the bend in the valley and up to the Rectory to call in on the Reverend Naismith-Parry and his wife. Adelaide Naismith-Parry was old and frail before her time. She had never got over her son's death and there were days when her mind became a little addled. For all that she was a sweet old lady and Eleanor was immensely fond of her. This morning, as she often did, she planned to prepare breakfast for the Rector and his wife before opening up the school. It was a morning ritual she looked forward to, not a chore.

It had been the Rector's suggestion that she take on the village school when the previous incumbent, a local woman, had migrated to Derby for a well-paid job in an aircraft factory in July 1941. Running the school, housekeeping for Adelaide, bringing up Johnny and Emmy and keeping the Gatekeeper's Lodge spick and span, Eleanor had made a new life in Lincolnshire. A busy and a full new life which despite widowhood had both purpose and meaning.

And hope.

On that Monday morning the mist drifted through the trees, veiling the outline of Ansham Hall and Eleanor stumbled into the cordon without knowing it. A taciturn man in a grey-blue, RAF Regiment greatcoat suddenly stepped out in front of her, blocking the way. His rifle was propped against a tree. He held out his arms, shivering.

"Sorry, Missus," he grunted. "You can't go this way."

"Why ever not?" Eleanor demanded, a little vexed.

"Crashed aircraft over there, see," explained the man, gesturing over his left shoulder with his thumb.

"But I need to get through to the Rectory?"

"Flight!" Shouted the guard into the fog and presently a glowering NCO emerged from the murk.

Eleanor repeated herself.

"I must get through. The Rector will be expecting me. He'll be worried!"

The Sergeant listened disinterestedly, refused to let her take another step along the path. She was on the verge of giving up, re-tracing her steps back to the cottage and going the long way around the hill when a familiar voice intervened.

"What's going on?"

The Sergeant and the guard jumped to attention as if their lives depended on it, and saluted crisply as the officer approached. Recognising the newcomer Eleanor breathed a heartfelt sigh of relief.

Adam Chantrey sauntered down the path. He was dressed in flying boots and a voluminous sheepskin jacket, with his cap pushed back on his head at a rakish angle. The greyness of the morning accentuated his pallor and the creeping exhaustion in his face. However, setting eyes on Eleanor his stern expression instantly mellowed into a surprised smile.

"Why, hello."

"Thank goodness for a friendly face," Eleanor smiled back. It was all she could do to stop herself giggling, laughing. She looked at the man and tingled with a half-forgotten, almost girlish delight. She lowered her eyes guiltily. "I can't seem to get anybody to understand that I've simply got to get through. The only other way round takes ages and we're already late. The Rector will be worried."

Jonathan and Emily, hanging on their mother's hands glanced curiously from face to face, not knowing what to make of things. Adam nodded to the NCO.

"It's all right, Flight. You can leave this to me."

"Yes, sir!"

"Come with me," Adam invited the woman. "There's no real danger. Not on this side of the wood." He extended a hand to Jonathan, who released his grip on his mother's hand and let himself be guided into the swirling mist. "We think a Canadian crew tried to land their Halifax on my runway last night. At least, we think that's what they were trying to do. We'll never know for sure. They landed in the trees about half-a-mile short of the perimeter fence. Bit of a mess, really."

"Oh, dear." From his tone she drew the obvious inference that the Canadians were dead.

"As I say, it's quite safe over this side of the woods. It's just that the drill is to keep everybody as far away as possible until we're absolutely sure it's safe. Better safe than sorry and all that guff." They walked on. The dampness dripped off the branches of the trees, underfoot leaves squelched muddily. "Look, I ought to have mentioned that I know your father. We're old, er, acquaintances. It was unforgivably remiss of me. How is the Prof, these days?"

"He works too hard," Eleanor complained. "He tires himself out. Apart from that he's as well as can be expected, I suppose."

"So you live just the other side of the hill?"

"Yes. You must come and visit us," Eleanor suggested, amazed by her own audacity. "I'm sure Father would love to see you," she added, quickly.

"If I can get away I shall certainly pay my respects. If I may?"

They had arrived at the gate to the Rectory.

"Father will look forward to it." Eleanor allowed her gaze to meet his as she spoke.

He grinned.

"And so shall I."

She watched him disappear into the mist.

After breakfast Eleanor went up to the Church Hall, readied it for the arrival of her class. Much later she looked in again on Adelaide as she prepared the Rector's lunch. She switched on the Home Service in time to listen to the news.

"Last night aircraft of Bomber Command were over Germany in great strength. The main objective was Kassel. Other aircraft attacked targets in the Ruhr, and mines were laid in enemy waters. Twenty-four of our aircraft are missing..."

Eleanor carried on peeling the potatoes. She tried not to think about the young men who had come all the way from Canada to fly with Bomber Command; only to perish in the night less than a mile from where she had slept safely in her bed.

Chapter 7

Monday 4th October, 1943
RAF Ansham Wolds, Lincolnshire

Adam was surprised and a little irritated when the Operations Room teleprinter clattered up the call to readiness. Bomber Command had mounted major operations on four of the last five nights. Admittedly, none of these operations had been all-Groups, maximum effort shows but many squadrons had participated in all of these attacks and would be badly in need of a respite.

Following the Kassel raid 647 Squadron's aircraft availability board - showing serviceable Lancasters available for operations that day - showed only 11 aircraft. A fall of 6 from the 17 available before the Hagen operation. This despite the fact that no aircraft had been lost in the three operations. The Squadron now had almost as many unserviceable aircraft as it had battle worthy.

"Group are only requesting six aircraft for tonight," Group Captain Alexander reported, reading directly from the print out. The teleprinter continued to clatter noisily in the background.

"Only six?"

The Old Man smiled, passed him the sheet of paper.

The static on the scrambler line to Bawtry Hall hissed as Adam waited for Pat Farlane to come to the phone.

"Not you again, old chap!" The Group Operations Officer complained, cheerfully. "Before you say another word, shut up and listened to Uncle Pat!"

Adam did as he was bade, keeping his powder dry.

"Nobody's been asked for more than six aircraft for tonight's show," Pat told him bluntly. "Group's been asked for fifty Lancs for some kind of spoof. Now get off the bloody line and stop wasting my time!"

The line went dead.

"What's the gen?" Alexander inquired, amused that Pat Farlane had hung up on Ansham Wolds' young lion before he could get a word in edgewise.

"Apparently, everybody's being asked for the same number of kites."

Mac had entered the bunker while Adam was on the phone to Group. He looked askance of his CO.

"For some kind of spoof," Adam shrugged.

Mac raised an eyebrow, otherwise said nothing. A couple of years ago a raid by 50 heavies would have constituted a major undertaking. Since then the bombing war had moved on. Nowadays, while a diversionary exercise involving 50 Lancasters was not without novelty, it seemed in no way excessive.

"I'm putting my head down for a couple of hours," Adam decided, suddenly very tired and disinclined to make small talk. "Mac, if you've got any sprogs you want to blood, tonight's the night."

The Flight Commander was thinking the same thought. In theory, these smaller scale operations ought to be fraught with risk. In practice, casualties tended to be low. When the fighter controllers identified a diversion for what it was, they ignored it, and concentrated on the main, larger bombing force. Some old lags had come to regard these spoofs as milk runs.

A few minutes after mid day the teleprinter reeled out the full battle order. 1 and 8 Groups were to send a force of at least 60 Lancasters to bomb Ludwigshafen while, simultaneously a Main Force drawn from 3, 4 and 6 Groups of over 400 Lancasters, Halifaxes and Stirlings would strike at Frankfurt-am-Main. Adam retired to his quarters, laid down fully clothed on his cot and the moment his head touched the pillow, slept. Normally a light sleeper, he was dead to the world, exhausted.

"You all right, Skipper?" This from Ben Hardiman, grinning down at him from his great height. Somebody had pulled the blinds, removed Adam's shoes, loosened his tunic buttons and spread a blanket over him to ward off the chill of the October day.

"I needed a nap," he muttered groggily, propping himself up on an elbow. He glanced at his watch. He had been asleep nearly three hours.

Ben shoved a steaming mug under his nose.

"Tea poisoned with a nip of something a tad more restorative," he confessed, pulling up a chair and dumping himself on it. "You're not going to keep this up indefinitely, are you?"

Adam sipped the tea. There was brandy in it.

"Keep what up?"

"You're worn out. You've got to pace yourself, Skipper."

"I'll get some shut-eye tonight."

"Make sure you do!" There was no rancour, no resentment in either man's words. The conversation was quiet, matter of fact, good-humoured.

"Things are coming right?" Adam offered. "The Squadron's coming round, don't you think?"

"Yes." Ben nodded.

"This is disgusting," Adam groaned, wrinkling his nose at the mug held shakily in his right hand.

"Barney's set the main crew briefing for sixteen hundred hours," the big man reported. "Look, Skipper," he went on. "I know you think Barney's a bit of a prat, but from what I've seen he seems to know what he's doing. Tell me to shove off if you want but you could do a lot worse than let him take a bit of the strain."

Adam scowled, half-heartedly.

"Just a thought," Ben chuckled. He had said his piece and that was an end of it. That was the way they operated. As likely as not they would die together and in most things, they understood each other perfectly. When they were alone, in private, Ben had leave to speak his mind whenever he thought fit; his friend reserved the right to ignore his advice and there were never any hard feelings. The big man got up, made as if to go.

"Ben," Adam called after his friend. "For what it's worth I don't think Barney's a prat. I just wish he'd stop behaving like one, that's all."

The other man half-smiled, slowly shook his head.

"Steady on, Skipper. You'll be giving him the benefit of the doubt next!"

Despite himself, Adam grinned broadly. When Ben was gone he got up, washed, shaved and donned the fresh uniform his batman had laid out for him.

His batman, a dapper, bespectacled man in his forties had quickly got used to his new master's idiosyncrasies. The man flitted around him silently, anticipated his every wish, unobtrusively, cheerfully. As if on cue Aircraftman Crawford materialised out of nowhere.

"May I be of assistance, sir?"

Adam gave in, let him re-knot his tie. "How long have you been at Ansham Wolds, Crawford?" He had scarcely said a word to the man since taking command of 647 Squadron. There had been so much to do. Too many new faces to put names to. Too many things to check, and re-check.

"Since January, sir. I came here with Wing-Commander Grant, sir. He was a fine gentleman. Very old-fashioned if you know what I mean." Henry Grant had been 647 Squadron's first CO. Crawford dusted off his charge's shoulders, stood back and surveyed his handiwork, then, spotting a minor imperfection he resumed his brushing.

"Were you with Wing-Commander Grant long?"

"Oh, yes, sir. You see, I was Mr. Grant's father's gentleman's gentleman for many, many years. When I got my call-up papers Mr. Grant senior said for me not to worry about a thing and next thing I knew I was reporting to Mr. Grant junior at Scampton. Yes, I was with Mr. Grant for nearly two years until..."

The Honourable Henry Jameson Grant had gone missing over Essen in April. Adam had had more than one run in with him in the old days. A decent enough fellow. A little straight-laced, not overly endowed with imagination. Henry Grant had arrived at Faldwell in the aftermath of the Wilhelmshaven debacle and taken over Peter Tomlinson's flight. A good golfer - at one time he was playing off a seven handicap - he recalled. Like Bert Fulshawe, on a bad day, Henry Grant was rather inclined to overdo the Hun-hating.

"But you've stayed on?" Adam observed. "You didn't ask to be re-assigned?"

"Oh, no, sir. Mr. Grant said to me: 'if anything happens to me,' that is, Mr. Grant, 'you just carry on as if nothing has happened.' So I've tried to do exactly that, if you catch my drift, sir. I mean, look at me, sir," he said, pausing, raised brush in hand. "What use would I be with a rifle in my hands? We each serve in our own way, sir."

Adam retrieved Rufus from the Adjutant's room where the Alsatian had taken up temporary residence and set off across the airfield on his daily constitutional. Overhead the clouds were high, the sky in places blue. The sun swept the vast open expanse of the aerodrome, warmed his bones and his soul. Ansham Wolds was becoming less strange with every passing day. Three ops flown without casualties - not so much as a scratch - was a better start than he had hoped for in his wildest dreams.

It would not last, nothing did. There would be a price to pay but he would deal with that when the time came.

The crews were flight testing their aircraft for the Ludwigshafen raid. He stood beside the controller's lorry, watched Q-Queenie race down the runway and lift into the air, raised an arm to wave her off as she roared past.   Other aircraft were rumbling onto the taxiway, lining up to take off.

Rufus ignored the spectacle of the Lancasters jockeying for takeoff.   He loped over to the controller's truck, cocked his leg against the rear offside wheel and proceeded to urinate on it.

Chapter 8

Peter Tilliard heard the bus long before it turned the corner. It groaned, chugged, and wheezed asthmatically up the hill around the back of the railway station. Evening was drawing in, dusk falling.

He had been waiting for over two hours, fretting, wondering if ACW Mills would actually turn up. A thousand things could have gone wrong since he had left a hastily written note for her: she might not even have got the note, or the duty roster might have been altered, Group Captain Alexander might have been called to an urgent conference at Group Headquarters, or decided on the spur of the moment to pay a social call on one of the neighbouring Station Masters. Anything could have gone wrong. His note might have been intercepted. The Senior WAAF was a dragon, infamous for her crusade against fraternization; making Ansham Wolds one of the few stations in 1 Group where the so-called "forty mile rule" had been religiously, rigidly, righteously enforced, at least in Bert Fulshawe's time. This was the pernicious rule which prevented a man - or for that matter, a woman - serving on a station less that forty miles from the matrimonial home. The Senior WAAF was a stickler for the letter of the regulations. A woman of unshakable convictions. Who knew what she was capable of when it came to safeguarding the reputations of *her* girls?

Tilliard took a deep breath, told himself to get a grip. ACW Mills would be on the next bus. Or not. Four buses had already come and gone. Perhaps, she had thought better of it? Decided it was too dicey and given the whole thing a miss? No, that was no way to think. ACW Mills struck him as a girl of a naturally plucky disposition, a free spirit. It was in her eyes, and in her smile. She was not the sort of girl likely to give up at the first hurdle.

He pulled his greatcoat close. Now that the weak autumnal sun was setting the chill was seeping into his bruises. He stepped onto the pavement outside the bus shelter. Stamping his feet he watched the bus crawling up the hill. Ever the optimist he thrust his hands deep into his pockets and crossed his fingers. If ACW Mills was not on this bus he would wait for the next, and then the next, and then the next. If necessary he would wait all night. Granted, it was hardly a foolproof plan but there was nothing else for it, except to wait.

The bus was dirty, crowded. It shuddered to a standstill, belching clouds of grey-blue smoke and passengers began to disembark. Men and women in RAF blue, chattering noisily. Tilliard tried not to look as fretful as he felt.

The next bus would be along in no time.

The Adjutant, Tom Villiers, had confided to him that the new Wingco had made him 'personally responsible' for laying on 'transport' whenever the crews were stood down. The old CO had never really troubled himself with 'non-ops' matters, and latterly, the lack of buses off station had been at the top of a long list of aircrew gripes. The new Wingco had homed in on the very 'non-ops' issues his predecessor had ignored with the same quiet, relentless energy he applied to operational matters. Consequently, it seemed Tom Villiers had free licence to organise as many buses as he thought fit and today, he had buses plying between the station and Scunthorpe, turn and turn about.

If ACW Mills was not on this bus, she might yet be on the next.

Or on the bus after that.

Tilliard forced himself to stand still. The sudden – almost magical - availability of reliable transport to Scunthorpe had done as much as anything to raise everybody's spirits, and no doubt, prompted numerous new liaisons, such as ACW Mills's and his.

He stood his ground; let the crowd wash around him.

Where was she?

Then he saw her, standing alone beside the bus, small and lost in the descending gloom. She was looking the other way.

"I say!" He called, voice cracking. "Over here!"

Her smile of relief melted a part of him.

"I didn't know if it was the right bus," she gasped. "Or where to get off. I'm sorry I'm late, you must have been awfully worried?"

"I'd have waited until midnight," he grinned.

She lowered her eyes, a little embarrassed.

"I did wonder," he confessed at a rush, "if you'd perhaps thought better of it. *This*, I mean. You're running a tremendous risk, I know."

The woman shrugged.

"I don't care."

Tilliard fought back the urge to sweep her up in his arms and hug her. In fact the only thing that stopped him was that he had never actually swept a girl up in his arms before. Chaps did that sort of thing all the time in the movies but that was in the movies, not real life. He gazed into her cornflower blue eyes and she gazed back.

"Gosh, I think you're tremendously brave."

"It's the first time I've been to Scunthorpe," she admitted. "I don't get on very well with the other girls, they always leave me behind. They think I'm a bit stuck up."

"That's jolly unfair."

"No," she laughed. "It's not, I'm afraid. I think they're a dreadful shower, actually!"

The man was laughing without knowing or caring why. "Goodness, I don't even know your first name?"

"Susan."

"Susan," he echoed, savouring it. "I knew it would be lovely name."

"Suzy. I insist that people I like call me Suzy."

"Suzy, then. And my name's Peter."

"I know. It suits you."

Tilliard was reeling. Suzy was swaddled in an over-sized greatcoat, fronds of straw blond hair flowing over her upturned collar, her cap jammed askew on her head. Her eyes twinkled with mischief, she was determined to enjoy every minute of this great new adventure.

"Isn't this exciting!" She exclaimed.

"I'm so pleased you came." The man saw she was shivering. "Let's get out of the cold. Find somewhere warm. There's a Fred Astaire and Ginger Rogers picture on at the Odeon."

"Actually, if you don't mind, I'd love a nice cup of tea."

"Oh, okay."

"You don't have to hide me away," Suzy admonished him, gently, tentatively. "Underneath this awful coat I'm in civvies. I look almost like a normal person. So you don't need to hide me away."

He blushed. "I'm sorry, I just thought..."

Suzy reached out and took his gloved hand in hers, squeezed it.

"You were just being thoughtful, I know. But I've got no intention of being ACW Mills when I'm with you. Leastways, not when we're off the station. If I've got to behave as if I'm the Groupie's little WAAF driver when we're together, there's really not much point in us doing this at all, is there?"

This took the man completely by surprise.

"Oh, dear, have I said the wrong thing?"

"Er, no. No," he stammered. "Not at all. Look, I know a little place across town. It's not very grand, but we can probably get something hot to eat. We can chat. If you don't mind walking. It's a fair old way."

She clasped his hand tightly.

"Lead on."

They walked for some minutes in silence, their pace unhurried, each reassessing the changed realities of their lives. By meeting today they had crossed a line that could never be un-crossed.

Time was short and they both knew it.

Chapter 9

Suzy had not slept a wink. Even now as she drove Group Captain Alexander and Wing-Commander Chantrey through the swampy, Nissen-hutted encampment below Bawtry Hall, she was mulling over the events of the previous evening.

Normally, she listened attentively to the Old Man's banter, learned many, many things the other girls would never learn about Ansham Wolds and the Squadron's distant battles.

Today, her passengers' conversation passed, by and large, over her head.

Today, unlike every previous day, the talk of aiming points, flak and fighter activity, marking patterns, bomb loads, creep back and the employment of navigation aids seemed to Suzy as far away as the German cities themselves. So distant as to be beyond her comprehension, outside her world, unreal. Today, it was as if the war had gone away for a day. Almost as if the war was nothing to do with her. Almost as if it was none of her business.

Her passengers chatted amicably. Mild-mannered, well-educated kindly gentle men urbanely discussing matters of the utmost violence: unspeakable violence waged against men and women, old and young, soldiers and civilians, factory workers, housewives and babes in arms alike. Unimaginable violence of which they were both key practitioners. It seemed so normal, so every day, banal. Fate had ordained that it was their duty to raze the cities of Greater Germany. Neither questioned the rightness of the cause, nor the means by which it was being pursued; they had a job to do and it was self-evidently a job that needed doing.

Somebody had to do it.

Suzy often found it hard to reconcile such conversations with the dreadful reality of what, nightly, *must* be happening over Germany. Sudden death rode in the bomber streams and stalked the ruins of the distant cities but her passengers might have been discussing a game of cricket.

The Old Man had been adept at keeping a lid on Wing-Commander Fulshawe's temper, at taking the sting out of his ire. The old Wingco had taken things rather religiously and tended to gloat when a raid went off well. The new Wingco was a quieter, more measured spirit, softly-spoken, almost schoolmasterish and Suzy suspected that the Station Master, accustomed to Wing-Commander Fulshawe's fervour, had not yet quite got the measure of the new man.

"Have you studied the reports on the Kassel show yet, sir?" Chantrey inquired, conversationally.

"Another show going off half-cock." Alexander grunted.

The crews had come home from Kassel with reports of concentrated bombing over the target and huge fires burning on the ground. Unfortunately, it seemed the Pathfinders might have overshot the aiming point by several miles. Much of the bombing had – once again - gone astray, leaving the major part of the city untouched.

"We don't know that for certain, sir," remarked the Wingco, respectfully. "If the chaps are right about the blind markers overshooting the AP again, a fair number of loads may well actually have hit the mark."

"*Creep* back is all very well," countered the Old Man with a sigh. "But there's no getting away from the fact most of the bombing probably went down in open country." Another sigh. "Pity our chaps missed the Frankfurt show. Fires still burning yesterday, according to the ops people. They say it may be the first time we've really hit the city hard."

Only 10 bombers had failed to return from Frankfurt-am-Main on Monday night. 647 Squadron - otherwise engaged on the Ludwigshafen spoof - had missed what sounded like a copybook raid. Photographic reconnaissance revealed that a great pall of smoke still shrouded the city 48 hours after the attack.

"Not for want of trying, sir."

"Indeed, not!"

The sun came out as Suzy dropped her charges in front of the Hall. They stepped out, straightened their uniforms. Suzy snapped to attention.

"We shall be at least a couple of hours, my dear," Alexander informed her. His tone was firm, solicitous. Fatherly. "Get into the warm. Pop over to the canteen and get yourself a cup of tea. I won't have you sitting out here in the cold waiting for us."

That was the thing about Group Captain Alexander. He was a gentleman to the core and considerate to a fault.

"Right, my boy," he said, turning to the Wingco. "Better not keep the AOC waiting, what."

Suzy saluted, watched the two men stride up the steps and disappear inside the building. Parking the car she walked around Bawtry Hall to the NAAFI where she sat by a window, alone, sipping a mug of tea, happily reprising her truly unforgettable evening in Scunthorpe with Peter Tilliard, her very own Flight-Lieutenant.

They had walked half-way across the town, eventually fetched up in a dingy, crowded café in a narrow cobbled street off the Lincoln Road.

'My first instructor at OTU,' Peter had recollected, 'took us on a flight up this way. He pointed at the steelworks and shouted something like: *See that, chaps? Bugger medieval Cathedrals! If the bloody Normans had really meant to build us some decent landmarks, they'd have made them glow in the dark!'*

Suzy had laughed. She had laughed a lot last night. Laughed until her sides hurt, and then laughed more. Peter was charming, modest, with a self-deprecating sense of humour that had instantly struck a chord. They had found a tiny table in a corner of the smoky room, shut out the babble of voices around them, talked about everything and nothing until it was time to run for the last bus back to the station. By then they had shared a pot of tea, eaten their austerity dinners; potatoes, a soupy looking vegetable and something that might once have been a portion of rabbit pie. And laughed and laughed.

Peter's father was a barrister, his mother had died when he was young. Tuberculosis, he said. He was the youngest of three brothers. Both his brothers were in the Army. The eldest, Edward, was in the Pay Corps, the middle brother, David, was a subaltern in the Middlesex Regiment. Edward was a bore, apparently. He took after their father. David was a life and soul of the party type. They were both much older, eleven and seven years respectively. Peter was twenty-three years old and had arrived in the RAF in January 1940 via Winchester College, Oxford and a short, unhappy sojourn in the Grenadier Guards.

'The Guards and I didn't get on at all,' he admitted, ruefully. 'I'm not a great fellow for drilling and bulling and all that tosh. So I volunteered for flying duties. It seemed like a jolly good wheeze at the time. I'd always wanted to fly, you see.'

'The Guards, I can't really imagine you in a bearskin?'

'Me neither! If the Guards hadn't taken a dislike to me I don't know what I'd have done. Anyway, after I volunteered for flying duties I was shipped off to Canada for basic training. The trip over was a bit dicey. A couple of the ships in our convoy were torpedoed but basic training was a piece of cake. When I survived that, they sent me on to advanced training, in Alberta. It's very, very flat out there. You wouldn't believe how flat it is! But that's another story. In all I was away from Blighty for nearly fifteen months. After OTU I got posted to Marston Grange near Lincoln. Onto Manchesters, you know, the two-engine version of the Lanc, just in time for the first of the thousand bomber raids on Cologne in May last year. Dreadful kites, Manchesters! Luckily, we converted to Lancs soon afterwards, thank goodness! After Marston Grange I was posted to Lindholme as an instructor.'

Suzy listened to his history with a mixture of amusement and a growing fascination. The fresh-faced, boyish, laughing-eyed man across the table was already, in Bomber Command terms, a hard-bitten old lag. He was only a year or two older than her and yet he had seen and experienced things she could only imagine, and then only in shades of grey. She found out that Peter did not smoke, and drank only in moderation.

'I can't drink. A pint or two and I am anybody's,' he confessed. 'It's not that I'm teetotal or anything, it's just that the stuff doesn't agree with me.'

Their voyage of discovery continued.

Finally, he had persuaded Suzy to talk about herself. She was just twenty-one, the younger of two siblings. Her brother, Alfred had gone into the bag just after Dunkirk, at Calais with the 51st Highland Division. So far as she knew he was alive, and as well as could be expected. Both her parents were similarly alive, and, she reported, also 'as well as could be expected'. Her father had been wounded more than once in the Great War but had never spoken of his experiences in the trenches. He was presently Headmaster of a small, obscure preparatory school in Shropshire. Her mother, a stoic, long-suffering lady some years younger than her husband had been horrified when her daughter had volunteered for service in the RAF.

'The WAAFs, darling? You could be sent anywhere!' Suzy exclaimed, mimicking her mother's startled indignation. 'I tried to explain to her that if I didn't volunteer for something interesting, then I'd probably get drafted onto a farm somewhere, or end up in some filthy old factory. But she wouldn't listen. So I told her that if she stopped me volunteering for the WAAFs I'd just wait until I was twenty-one and do it anyway.'

'It must have been a terrible wrench, leaving home?' The man prompted.

'No, not really.'

'Surely, you must have had a boyfriend. Or somebody special?'

'No,' she smiled. 'Mother wouldn't have had that!'

'There must have been somebody?' Peter Tilliard had insisted, with what had seemed like genuine incredulity.

'Nobody,' she had declared, lowering her gaze.

'So, how did you end up at Ansham Wolds?'

'Alfie used to have this old Morris and he taught me how to drive when I was young, about fourteen. When the RAF found out I could drive, they posted me to Group as a driver and a couple of days later I got posted to Ansham Wolds. When I arrived here they heard my posh accent, well, it's not really that posh but people think it is posh, if you see what I mean, and they detailed me as the Groupie's regular driver. Alfie always used to say *don't worry about Suzy, Mother, she usually ends up on her feet.* And I usually do.'

They had walked back across the city as the public houses were emptying onto the streets. Having planned to catch separate buses they had forgotten themselves and completely lost track of time. They would have to pretend to be strangers on the last bus and attempt to melt into the crowd.

In the event their plan had come to nought.

Outside *The Liberty* they passed a group of men

huddled over a crumpled figure on the ground. Recognising several of the men as members of the Wingco's crew, Peter Tilliard had stopped, whispered to Suzy that it would be best if she waited across the other side of the street while he investigated. The man on the ground turned out to be the Wingco's rear gunner, Taffy Davies.

'What's the problem, chaps?' Tilliard had demanded, radiating calm authority and fixing his eye on the tall, swaying figure of Bob Marshall.

'Er, Taffy's not too good, sir,' slurred the boy gunner.

'Picked a fight with a couple of brown types, sir,' supplemented Bert Pound. He was very drunk, kept upright only by the supporting hands of his friends.

Tilliard frowned, and crouched down over the prostrate gunner.

'Brown types, eh?' He echoed. He had walked half-way across Lincoln that night without laying eyes on a single soldier. It was more likely that the gunner had had a run in with several of B Flight's finest. Apart from the affable Ben Hardiman, the Wingco's crew had made no secret of the fact they regarded themselves as being a cut above the rest. Somebody, it seemed, had decided to put the newcomers in their place.

'Yes, sir.'

Tilliard shook his head.

'Davies! Can you hear me?' The man on the ground groaned. 'Try and sit up man!' To his surprise the gunner stirred, raised himself onto an unsteady elbow. His nose was bleeding profusely, his face puffy, beginning to swell. Vomit dribbled down his tunic front. 'Didn't any of you chaps do anything to stop this?'

'Taffy went for a piss, sir. We came out as soon as we heard the rumpus. The bastards buggered off as soon as they saw us,' this from an unknown man behind Marshall's shoulder, it might have been Ted Hallowes.

'Never mind. Give him a hand. Let's see if we can

get him on his feet.'

The gunner's friends hauled him vertical, held him while he dazedly surveyed his surroundings.

'Fucking officers...' The Welshman muttered, spitting out blood and a broken tooth. 'Fucking officers...'

'See if he can walk.' The little man's legs instantly buckled beneath him. 'You'll have to carry him back to the bus.'

'Shit! That's blown it!' Two policemen were approaching. 'Bandits at three o'clock!' The men holding Taffy Davies cursed vociferously.

Tilliard straightened to his full height of six foot and the best part of an inch. He made no attempt to conceal his mounting displeasure.

'Right, you lot make sure Davies gets back to the station!' He barked. 'And for goodness sake clean him up a bit! Go on, get to it!'

'Yes, sir...' Chorused the drunks.

'What about the rossers, sir?'

'I'll deal with the police!'

'What's going on?' Suzy had asked, crossing the street as the band of drunken aircrew stumbled past her into the gloom half-carrying, half-dragging the senseless gunner.

'It seems the Wingco's rear-gunner got into a fight,' Tilliard explained, taking her hand in his as they moved to intercept the approaching constables.

'What's going on here, sir,' asked the larger of the two very large, somewhat sour-faced constables. Both policemen eyed the aircrew swaying down the street in the middle distance.

'One of *my* gunners has had a tad too much to drink, Constable,' Tilliard replied, cheerfully. '*My* chaps are looking after him. Nothing for you to be concerned about.'

'We'll be the judge of that, sir!'

'Of course. The chaps have been out celebrating. The man concerned shot down a Messerschmitt 110 the other night and saved *all* our lives. I'm not a drinker myself, but in my book I think that calls for a little celebration. Don't you? Besides, I wasn't aware that there had been a breach of the peace. Or a complaint?'

The constables viewed him thoughtfully, their stare moving from the man to the woman and back to the man. Tilliard had assumed a mask of amiable disdain. Suzy had smiled, fluttered her eyelids. While the policemen pondered the situation and their options, Taffy Davies was dragged around the corner, safely out of sight. This seemed to make up their minds.

'Well, sir. No harm done, then. You'll be wanting to be on your way, I expect.'

'Yes, Officer. Good night.'

Tilliard had led Suzy away.

'I'm sorry about that. I couldn't walk on by.'

'What would the police have done?'

'Locked them all up for the night. Bounced one or two of the chaps around the cells. That seems to be the normal drill. I've heard some bad stories.'

If a chap got shot down over Germany he could invoke the protection of the Geneva Convention; if he got on the wrong side of the law in Scunthorpe, or for that matter anywhere else in Lincolnshire he was liable to be roughed up by the local constabulary. It was a funny old world.

'That's terrible,' Suzy had protested, a little shocked. They had scurried along in silence for some minutes. 'We'll all be on the same bus,' she had pointed out. 'They'll have seen us together. They'll put two and two together.'

'I know. I'm sorry, it can't be helped.'

'It's all right, I don't care.'

He had stopped and she had looked up into his face.

'Suzy. May I kiss you?'

At that moment she was his to do with as he wished. She longed for him to sweep her up in his arms.

'Of course you can, silly!'

Chapter 10

Thursday 7th October, 1943
RAF Ansham Wolds, Lincolnshire

Sergeant Pilot Percival and his fresh-faced crew awaited Peter Tilliard under the nose of P-Popsie. The commander of Ansham Wolds's conversion flight ran a jaundiced eye over his charges, trying very, very hard to collect his thoughts. This morning his thoughts were distracted, elsewhere. Suzy's cornflower blue eyes were with him every step he took, and her giggle took him unawares at every turn. He shook his head.

"Hello, chaps."

"Good morning, sir..." The sprogs replied, raggedly in chorus.

Tilliard sighed. Last night he had sent Suzy on ahead so she could get onto the bus alone. The Wingco's crew were old lags, there would be no problem with them. But as for the other people hanging around outside *The Liberty*, any one of them might report him and Suzy to the Station Master. Or worse, to the Senior WAAF. Nevertheless, he had sent Suzy on ahead. There was no point flaunting their affair.

To call it an 'affair' sounded a little odd, after all they had only gone out once and throughout they had behaved most properly. Until they had kissed, anyway. Her mouth, warm, soft, open had met his, her lips had brushed and then pressed against his, and lingered long, moistly. His legs had turned to rubber, his head had spun and he had suddenly discovered the difference between a friendship and having 'an affair'.

The sprogs waited, patiently. They waited in silence. Waited in a very, very particular respectful silence thinking absolutely nothing untoward of their instructor's apparent distraction. Their instructor was, after all, an ops man who had logged hundreds of hours on four-engine heavies. Moreover, their instructor had flown in the bomber streams to Germany more than thirty times and lived to tell the tale. Ops men were special, especially the old lags, a different breed, creatures beyond their ken, strangers to them. To the sprogs the brotherhood of ops men to which they aspired remained to them a secret society, and its members closed books.

So, they waited respectfully until their instructor remembered where he was and more importantly, why he was there.

"Right," Tilliard growled, reluctantly relegating Suzy to the back of his mind. He needed to be on the ball this morning because unless he was on top of his form any one of the seven sprogs standing - innocently, harmlessly - before him was perfectly capable of doing something unbelievably stupid and getting him killed. Getting killed was always on the agenda when you were flying with sprogs. Particularly when you were flying with sprogs who had next to no flying hours on Lancs.

"Right, perhaps you'd like to introduce me to the chaps, Percival. I always like to know into whose hands I'm putting my life, what!"

Increasingly, Bomber Command's war was fought by men in their late teens and early twenties: boys plucked from schools, youths from dreary offices, young men eager to escape from mills, mines and factories. Few aircrew would have laid eyes on a real aeroplane before the war and but for the coming of the war, would probably never have had the opportunity to fly. Many of the men who flew Bomber Command's heavies would have learned to fly, like Tilliard himself, before they had learned to drive a car. Aircrew were volunteers to a man. Some had volunteered for flying duties to avoid the foot-slogging lot of the infantryman, a few because they genuinely believed the war might be won or lost in the air. Most had volunteered for no better reason than that they wanted to fly. The romance of flight was like a spider's web drawing the idealistic youth of the Empire into the great maw of a remorseless, insatiable beast. Although some men specifically requested, even demanded, a posting to Bomber Command, the vast majority of aircrew arrived in the bomber fiefdom by default, the victims of Air Ministry bureaucracy. But once cast upon the shore of one of Bomber Command's far-flung islands a man's fate was by and large, in the lap of the gods.

The introductions over, Tilliard wasted no time.

"Today," he declared, "we're going up to Lindisfarne on a navigation exercise. If everything goes to plan, on the way back we will make a detour to Marton Heath and drop a couple of practice bombs. Just so there is no misunderstanding, the purpose of this exercise is for me to assess what, if any, progress you chaps have made since you got here and to consider whether or not you should be let loose on ops. To make this as realistic as possible I intend to be a *hands-off* passenger."

He didn't say: *unless, of course, one of you does something that's likely to get us all killed.* That was the sort of thing a chap did not usually say out loud on occasions like this; the sprogs were nervous enough as it was.

At the Wingco's instigation, all sprog crews now had to survive a gruelling *corkscrew run* before they graduated onto the Squadron's order of battle. Today's flight was to assess whether Sergeant Pilot Percival's crew was sufficiently competent to be allowed to undertake a *corkscrew run.*

'We must try to do our best by our sprogs, Peter,' Chantrey had insisted, with that quiet, implacable vehemence of his that took a man's breath away. 'We must do what we can to give them hope. They must be given a fighting chance to come through. I won't have our sprogs thrown to the wolves. I won't have it!'

That was the thing about the Wingco, whoever you were: flight-commander or grease monkey, if you were on *his* Squadron he was on your side and woe-betide anybody who forgot it. Once again, Tilliard had briefly lost his train of thought.

Suzy's blue eyes were laughing...

A sprog gleaned his first inkling of what awaited him when he reported to his Operational Training Unit. By the time he got to an OTU his training was supposedly coming to an end after at least one, and for a pilot up to two years of interminable graft. At any stage in his training a man could have been unceremoniously thrown off his course and returned to ground duties. To have made it as far as an OTU was no mean achievement, eloquent testimony that a man was among the best and the brightest of his peers. It was at his OTU that a man first encountered significant numbers of *survivors*. The survivors were not of course, called 'survivors'; Bomber Command elected to classify them as 'instructors'.

Tilliard donned his grimmest face.

The nucleus of this particular sprog crew had, like most crews, coalesced at OTU: pilot, navigator, engineer, bomb-aimer and wireless operator deciding, informally, casually amongst themselves that they would fly - and therefore most likely, die - together. The two gunners had been assigned at Ansham Wolds.

At OTUs rumours of the Main Force's distant war with the cities filtered back to the sprogs. Rumours cloaked reality, and in any event, the nature of the war with the cities was ever-changing. Tactical and scientific innovations, not to mention the vagaries of the weather, continually shifted the balance of advantage, randomly tilting the odds in the lottery of life and death. Flying ops was as much Russian Roulette as a science, and experience of prevailing operational conditions was always a currency liable to swift and brutal debasement.

"Before we mount up, let's recap *Tilliard's law*!"

The OTUs were sending them children, boys who would not be out of place in any pre-war school's first eleven.

"One: if I tell you to do something you do it immediately! Two: if I tell you to do something you do it without hesitation! Three: if I tell you to do something you do it without question! Clear?"

The sprogs had heard it before. They grinned, nodded jerkily.

"Yes, sir!" They acknowledged in unison.

It was cold, there was rain in the air. Time was pressing.

The sprogs had done the bulk of their training on worn out, twin-engine Vickers Wellingtons. Designed by the redoubtable Barnes Wallis - of Dam busters' bouncing bomb fame - the 'Wimpey' had been a mainstay of Bomber Command for the first two years of the war. The Wellington was a sturdy, stable, forgiving aircraft to fly. Unfortunately, as a training aircraft for men destined to fly in the bomber streams to Germany in this, the fifth year of the war, the trusty old Wellington had one rather large and glaringly obvious drawback. The Main Force comprised *four-engine* Lancasters, Halifaxes and Stirlings.

Percival and his crew had been posted direct to 647 Squadron for conversion to the type of aircraft it was to fly in battle. Some crews, the lucky few, passed through one of the newly formed Heavy Conversion Units, like the one at Lindholme. Currently, Lindholme remained the only HCU equipped with Lancasters, the others still flew Stirlings. After a month at Ansham Wolds Sergeant Pilot Percival still had less than twenty hours flying experience on Lancasters.

"One last thing," Tilliard announced bleakly, as the rain began to fall.

The sprogs craned forward, expectantly.

Upon joining an operational squadron the veil soon

fell from a sprog's eyes. On the squadrons the mill ground, the chop-rate rose and fell, faces came and went, heavies went missing in the night, crashed, ditched, or limped home horribly mauled. Training accidents were commonplace as inexperienced crews suddenly found themselves flying over-loaded aircraft in all weathers. Wisely, on the squadrons the odds against survival were rarely discussed. Each man was condemned to accomplish 30 round trips to Germany or perish in the attempt, and the plain fact of the matter was that death, wounding or imprisonment awaited the majority and everybody knew it. In the unlikely event a man survived his first tour of 30 ops he earned a six month respite, after which he could be called back to operations at any time and asked to do it all over again. Statistically, in the war to date, the odds of surviving two tours unscathed were roughly of the order of six to one: against.

Such was the reality of flying with Bomber Command.

"Good luck, chaps."

Tilliard waved for the sprogs to mount up, hung back and watched them clamber into the big black bomber. Forty percent of Main Force casualties were suffered by crews on their first half-a-dozen ops. Nobody would ever know for sure how many men had gone to their deaths for the want of half-way adequate operational training. The OTU's churned out crews who could fly a bomber with a modicum of competence, no more or no less. Unfortunately, survival over Germany demanded a great deal more. Sprog crews who spent all their time simply keeping their aircraft airborne had no time to spare for the observance of the hundred and one ever changing rules of life and death over Germany. Old lags like Peter Tilliard never failed to be amazed by the ways sprogs found to get themselves killed.

One last look around and Tilliard followed the sprogs

up the ladder into the bomber. Nothing scared him quite
so much as flying with sprogs.

Nothing.

Chapter 11

Saturday 9th October, 1943
RAF Ansham Wolds, Lincolnshire

Suzy spied Peter Tilliard from afar as dusk settled over the fields. He was striding out with the Wingco's German Shepherd loping at his heels on a long leash. Behind him the distant hangars and administration huts merged with the darkening horizon. At her back the wind rustled through the trees flanking the perimeter fence. Stepping out into the open she stamped her feet on the cold tarmac of Dispersal 12.

The man waved and quickened his step.

It was too risky to meet again in Scunthorpe, at least in the near future. The legend of how Peter had stepped in to save the Wingco's crew from a night in *Stalag Luft Scunthorpe* was all round the aerodrome. Each time she heard the story it had acquired a new and even more outlandish embellishment. Thus far, it seemed as if she had remained anonymous, miraculously unassociated with the drama. However, just before departing the Waafery that afternoon she had inadvertently bitten her lip when she overheard a girl in her dormitory gossiping about Peter having been with 'some tart' outside *The Liberty*.

"I was hoping to have you to myself," Suzy laughed nervously, looking at Rufus.

"Ah, yes. I thought it might look a bit odd if I just wandered off into the distance," he explained. "But with this chap in tow nobody bats an eyelid."

They walked on. "The hole in the fence is supposed to be a bit further along, in the trees," she reported. The drizzle was blowing on the wind.

"Damn, I think it's going to tip down any minute," Tilliard observed, viewing the skies.

They made their way through the wood until they

came upon the tall perimeter fence.

"I think we've forgotten something," Suzy decided, stopping abruptly under a tree whose spreading branches still retained a thick thatch of leaves.

"What's that?"

"Come here!" She giggled, taking his arm and drawing him close. "I think I deserve a kiss for coming all the way out here, don't you?"

The man laughed, took her in his arms, lifted her off her feet momentarily as he planted a kiss on her lips. She kissed him back hard, lips parted and he followed her lead.

"Where did you say this hole in the fence is?" He gasped, coming up for air.

"Not far." She clasped his hand and they set off deeper into the trees.

Five minutes later they reached the place in the perimeter where the day before there had been a gaping hole in the high, wire-mesh fence. The ground around where the hole had been was muddy, trampled from where the boots of the repair crew had been working, probably as recently as that morning.

"Damn!" Tilliard groaned.

The repaired fence was unwelcome confirmation that the Wingco's very public, and by all accounts, explosive public 'chivvying along' of the Guard Flight Commander on the tarmac outside the control tower earlier in the week had had the desired result. Mac had witnessed the short, sharp interview, and reported the incident blow by blow to his old lags with enormous relish. The CO had torn the poor fellow off a fearful strip, ordering him in no uncertain terms to buck up his ideas.

The Guard Flight Commander was in good company. The persistent shortage of serviceable aircraft had positively enraged the Wingco. He was on the war path, ruthlessly geeing up Ansham Wolds' section heads.

'The new Wingco's gone through the ops team like a

dose of salts!' One old lag had chortled in the Mess the previous day. The crews were taking an undisguised and unashamedly perverse delight in the Wingco's brutal weeding out of the Squadron's dead wood. So far as the crews were concerned the 'cull' was long overdue. Whereas the old Wingco had cracked down on the crews whenever they reported mechanical problems while largely leaving the engineering section to its own devices, Chantrey, notwithstanding his promise 'not to tolerate fringe merchants' had made it abundantly clear that nobody was going to be accused of being a 'fringe merchant' without very, very good cause. So, having posted a new standing order to the effect that any aircraft returning early from an operation was to be subjected to an exhaustive mechanical inspection, he had simultaneously instigated a root and branch reorganisation of the engineering section.

Overnight, every aircraft had acquired its own dedicated 'core' maintenance crew. Lines of responsibility had been redrawn and for the first time in months everybody – from the lowliest erk to the oldest lag, from the WAAFs in the NAAFI to department heads, from the girl who tore the orders off the Ops Room teleprinter to Barney Knight, the Squadron's second-in-command - knew exactly where they stood. The new Wingco radiated an inner strength and confidence that infected every part of the Squadron but anybody not pulling their weight could expect to feel the full force of his wrath, which Tilliard was coming to understand was of the terrible, slow-burning, cold-blooded, calculating variety. Adam Chantrey never seemed to raise his voice, never seemed to lose his rag but woe betide anybody caught in his sights. Several 647 Squadron stalwarts had already departed: the old bombing leader, an amiable buffoon; the senior engineering officer; the operations officer and his deputy, both gung ho, life and soul of the Mess types. All gone, posted within hours, ruthlessly swept away by the new broom with the changes rubber-stamped by the Station Master without, apparently, so much as the batting of an eyelid.

Most of the departees had been replaced by younger blood, promoted from within the fold. Which was unusual. When a Squadron got a bad name for itself, Group invariably preferred to bring in new men. Chantrey had told his Flight Commanders that he was having none of that. 647 Squadron had had a bad run but it was nothing that could not be sorted out locally. He had paused to take stock of the situation in his first forty-eight hours at Ansham Wolds, and having given the existing crews a vote of confidence, unequivocally decided to place his trust in the crews to hand. Against the odds, in less than a fortnight 647 Squadron had been transformed from a demoralised shambles into something akin to the *press on* fighting unit it had been the previous Spring. The sprogs were in awe of the Wingco, and some of the older hands, too. Even Barney Knight's old lags pricked up their ears and listened, hard, when the CO spoke because suddenly, flying ops had ceased to be the death sentence it had become in the final throes of Bert Fulshawe's tenure.

Which was all well and good but no matter how hard Tilliard stared at the perimeter fence yesterday's gaping hole stubbornly refused to re-open.

Suzy sighed. She thought about stamping her feet but in the end refrained from so doing. The ground was wet and muddy and she would only have splashed her shoes. Her innocent little assignation with Peter Tilliard was over before it had begun and worse, every moment they remained together they risked discovery.

"Oh, well that's that," Tilliard said, admitting defeat. "I'm sorry, but we better make our way back to civilisation. If we run into anybody we'll have to tell them you were walking Rufus." The rain poured down mercilessly. "I'm going to have to try and get a car," he declared, thinking out aloud. "Otherwise this sort of thing is liable to happen to us all the time."

"Can you afford it?"

"No. Not really."

"Well, how are you going to get hold of a car, then?"

"I don't know. But I will. I'll find a way!"

Suzy believed him.

They were both soaked to the skin by the time they reached the hangars. The woman was shivering as she trudged off back to the Waafery. By then the cold and the wet had completely drowned the fleeting romance of their kiss in the woods.

Tilliard watched her go. They had to be better organised; things needed to be properly planned. Meeting on the Station was reckless. Stupid. It would be bad enough to be caught together, but to be caught within the bounds of the aerodrome would be disastrous. Especially for Suzy. The worst they could do to him was rap his knuckles, transfer him to another Squadron but given half a chance they would throw the book – probably the whole library - at Suzy.

That would never do.

Suzy arrived back at the Waafery bedraggled and downcast to be greeted by a worrying summons from the Senior WAAF. Without pausing to change out of her wet uniform and with an awful, sinking feeling in the pit of her stomach she hurried through the rain to the Flight Office where the Senior WAAF held court in the coldest, dankest corner of the big Nissen Hut. Stepping between the puddles she steeled herself for the worst.

They had been discovered!

Suzy tried to think of an innocent explanation but gave up almost immediately. Better by far to deny everything, play dumb, act ignorant. She hated the idea of disowning Peter, hated the thought of lying about him but there was no choice.

The Senior WAAF was a stout, dour woman in her

fifties who made a point of individually speaking to every woman posted to Ansham Wolds about the 'dangers' and 'pitfalls' of 'wartime romances' in general and 'wartime romances with aircrew' in particular. The first hint of scandal was sufficient – without exception since there was no possibility of mitigating circumstances - to see a woman transferred off the station. The Senior WAAF did not look up when Suzy knocked and entered the room.

"ACW Mills reporting as ordered, Ma'am."

The older woman put down her pen, retrieved a manila file from her in tray, opened it slowly, thoughtfully. Suzy was trembling, now. The Senior WAAF sighed portentously.

"Ah, yes. Mills. At the suggestion of Group Captain Alexander I've recommended that your name be put forward for a commission, young lady."

Suzy froze, too stunned to reply.

"Well?" Inquired the Senior WAAF

"Er, thank you, Ma'am."

Inexplicably, the older woman smiled a smile that was half-way towards being maternal. This further unnerved Suzy.

"A bright girl like you is wasted in the motor pool. The Station Master is very keen to see your name go forward. Of course, it's entirely up to you. Would you like a little time to consider matters?"

Suzy was grateful to clutch at any straw.

"Yes please, Ma'am."

The Senior WAAF became aware that the younger woman was soaking wet. Water dripped steadily from her tunic and skirt, forming a small, spreading puddle on the floor.

"Very well. In the meantime, for goodness sake get out of those wet clothes before you catch your death!"

Chapter 12

Saturday 9th October, 1943
The Rectory, Ansham Wolds, Lincolnshire

Adam braked the Bentley to a squealing halt in the lane outside the Rectory. High on the hill the square Norman tower of St Paul's Church was silhouetted against the threatening overcast. The Rectory was an ancient, ivy-infested, thatched cottage. There were thorny bushes, festooned with red rosehips in the garden, flowerless hanging baskets by the door. Autumn was turning towards winter.

Following two nights of intensive operations the weather had grounded 1 Group's Lancasters. But not before Ansham Wolds' run of good fortune had ended. The 6 aircraft sent to Ludwigshafen - including 3 sprog crews making operational debuts - at the beginning of the week had returned safely. Likewise, the 11 crews participating in the Lancaster Force attack on Stuttgart on Thursday. However, last night's attack on Hanover signified a return to business as usual. One of the 27 missing heavies was S-Sugar. Nor was S-Sugar the Squadron's only casualty. A fighter attack over the target had killed Q-Queenie's bomb-aimer and wounded two other crew members.

It was the Rector, the Reverend Simon Naismith-Parry, who answered the door. The younger man took off his cap, viewed the beanpole, stooped man of somewhat austere visage and rheumy, sad eyes.

"Good afternoon, sir," He began. "I'm Wing-Commander Chantrey. I'm the CO of 647 Squadron. Would it be all right if I came in? I hope I haven't come and an inconvenient time?"

Group Captain Alexander had cautioned Adam that the Rector entertained 'certain deeply felt reservations' about the way Bomber Command presently waged its war. The Station Master's parting advice had been: 'He's a charming fellow, but forewarned is forearmed, what! Try to be diplomatic, there's a good man!'

Although Adam was braced for a prickly, awkward reception he need not have worried. The Rector's severe expression instantly dissolved into a welcoming smile.

"Inconvenient? Of course it isn't inconvenient! Goodness me, no! Please, do come in, Wing-Commander. My wife will be so pleased, she's been so looking forward to meeting you, young man. And, I must confess, so have I."

"Really, sir?" Adam murmured, his fears confounded.

The Rector drew him inside.

"Adelaide, my dear! We have a visitor!" He called into the warm, friendly depths of the cottage. "Come and see who has come to visit us!"

The Rector's wife smiled up at her guest, took his right hand in her own dry, frail hands. "Oh, what a nice surprise. We've heard so much about you, Wing-Commander. Haven't we, Simon?"

"Indeed, we have," laughed the old man. "I'm being most remiss. Do forgive me, Wing-Commander. Let me introduce you to my wife, Adelaide."

"How do you do, Mrs. Naismith-Parry," Adam muttered, overwhelmed.

"You must call me Adelaide," insisted the Rector's wife in a tone which brooked no dissent. "And you will stay for tea, won't you?"

Adam shifted uncomfortably. "That's awfully decent of you. I wouldn't like to put you to any bother on my account."

It was at this point that the Rector came to his rescue.

"Now, now, my dear. The Wing-Commander is an extremely busy man. And I'm thinking that perhaps he has something he would like to discuss with me?"

"Actually, yes, sir."

The Rector took him by the elbow. "Shall we go through to the study," he suggested, tactfully. "If you'll excuse us, my dear."

The small, oak-beamed study was walled with countless books. A few – a miniscule minority - were obviously theological works, the overwhelming majority were novels or sporting titles. The Reverend Naismith-Parry had a partiality for detective fiction and cricket books. Tall windows opened onto a narrow garden enclosed by a low stone wall. The air was musty, reminiscent of the atmosphere one might encounter in some neglected corner of an antiquarian bookshop. Adam's eye ranged along the shelves, pausing here and there to note a title. He whistled softly, impressed.

"My word, you've quite a library, sir."

"Yes, I suppose I have." The old man's face lit up, then he was thoughtful. "I find solitude with my books. Please, take a seat." He guided his guest to an ancient, threadbare armchair by the window. Outside, trees prematurely shorn of their leaves by the recent heavy rain jutted barrenly out of the hillside, their fallen leaves spread like a pall upon the land, and their branches a hundred different kinds of gallows. The Reverend Naismith-Parry sat down at his desk, a gentle, quixotic smile playing on his thin lips. "I think a man needs solitude from time to time. Without solitude he has no opportunity to look into himself. Nor an opportunity to make his peace with whatever gods he chooses to place his faith in."

Adam looked up.

"Or, to make one's peace with what one must do," he offered, exchanging one thought for another.

"Perhaps," the old man conceded, clasping his hands on his lap. "You'll be a Cambridge man?"

"Er, yes."

"A guess," the Rector confessed. "And a classics

man, I dare say?"

Adam nodded. "For my many sins, sir."

"And now you command a bomber squadron," the old man, remarked. "We live in strange times, do we not?" The Rector liberated a pipe from a rack on the window ledge, packed it with tobacco from a pouch he retrieved from an unseen desk drawer. He struck a match. "Forgive me, Wing-Commander. Please, smoke if you wish." He puffed contentedly, sat back, gazed at his guest. "Mind you, things will be different after the war. People sometimes forget that all wars come to an end."

Adam withdrew a cigarette from his silver case, accepted the proffered lighted match. The war of which the Rector spoke so distantly, so abstractly, had torn his and countless other families apart and killed or maimed, inwardly or outwardly, just about all his friends.

"It'll end when we've won it," he retorted, mildly.

"I prattle somewhat," smiled the old man. "A consequence of my advancing years, so I'm told." The famous Wing-Commander's reputation came before him and now that he had met him the Rector saw that much of what he had heard was firmly rooted in the truth. He noted the ribbons of the Distinguished Service Order and the Distinguished Flying Cross on his visitor's breast below the faded pilot's wings. Noted also the weariness in his face and the hollowness in his eyes; a hollowness and a strange, inexplicable serenity for he saw before him a man old before his time. "It is said," he went on, "that I hold certain views about the way the RAF conducts the bombing campaign against Germany."

Adam said nothing.

The Rector sighed and the slackness in his face betrayed every day of his sixty-eight years. "I have never denied that I hold these views. Unfortunately, the very fact that I hold these views has been taken to imply that, in some sense, I harbour a personal animosity towards the men and women serving here in Ansham Wolds.

Please believe me when I say that nothing could be further from my heart, Wing-Commander. Nothing."

Adam remained silent.

The old man shrugged, sadly.

"Oh, dear. You don't approve of me, do you, Wing-Commander?"

"May I speak frankly, sir?"

"Of course."

"I find it hard to believe that a man of the cloth such as yourself cannot entertain the precept of righteous anger."

This intrigued the old man.

"Righteous anger. Indeed!"

Adam shrugged.

"Yes, I think that's what I'd call it. I'm not a particularly religious chap but I certainly believe in righteous anger. And because I believe in righteous anger I believe in what we're doing and in the absolute necessity of doing it."

The Rector puffed at his pipe. Chantrey was every bit the unusual, very remarkable young man that his late friend, Bert Fulshawe, had often described. Bert had always spoken of him as if he was a younger brother whose career and character were sources of immense and unashamedly filial pride. Bert, of course, had been a man who wore his passions on his sleeve, whereas the man who had stepped into his shoes was evidently a more cerebral creature, whom even on first acquaintance, gave every indication that he was a man cast from a metal tempered in a still fiercer flame.

"The 'it' being the indiscriminate bombing of the German civilian population?" The Rector prompted. When Adam refused to take the bait the old man gave in gracefully. "Forgive me. That was unfair."

Adam stared through the window at the gaunt trees shivering in the wind. The veil had fallen from his eyes long ago. The RAF had sent him to Ansham Wolds to bomb men, women and children, fit or infirm, soldiers, war workers and babes in arms alike. That was his job, his *duty*, and he made no bones about it. He did not need a lecture on morality to know *per se* that what he was doing was wrong. Of course it was wrong. Morally indefensible, in fact. However, while the Rector was free to moralise in a vacuum and to pretend the horrors of the world were mere chimeras, he could not. The Luftwaffe had sown the seeds - murdered tens of thousands of defenceless women and children in Warsaw, Rotterdam, London, Coventry and in a score of other British cities - now the Third Reich was reaping the whirlwind.

"No, not unfair," he said, conceding ground even as he sought to draw a line in the sand. "Perfectly fair, actually. But I don't think that's the point."

"Ah, the terrible things our enemies make us do?"

Adam allowed himself the ghost of a smile.

"Something like that, sir."

The Reverend Naismith-Parry was itching to press him further even though to have done so would have been unspeakably rude, impolite, and unforgivably crass.

"You remind me of my son, Wing-Commander. He was killed in a training accident. He was terribly burned. They said it was a mercy that he did not live. That was over a year ago, now. He flew Stirlings. 'A gentleman's aircraft' he used to say."

"I'm sorry, sir. I didn't know."

"Nevertheless," the Rector declared, "I'm afraid I can't subscribe to righteous anger. Forgiveness, yes. Anger, never."

Adam scratched his head. "We shall have to agree to differ, sir."

"So it would seem. But you didn't come here to debate metaphysics?"

"No, sir. A bomb-aimer on one of my aircraft was

killed over Hanover last night. I gather that in the past the Adjutant has always made the necessary arrangements but when one of my people is killed in action I prefer, whenever possible, to personally oversee the funeral arrangements. I am also of the view that when a man is killed flying from Ansham Wolds it is not just an RAF matter but a thing that should rightfully be shared with the wider community, in this case, with the whole village."

The Rector nodded, suggested either Tuesday or Wednesday the following week as days which might be set aside for the funeral.

"Tuesday," Adam decided.

"You're absolutely right, of course. These sad events ought to bring everybody together." Matters quickly concluded, the Rector remembered his manners. "Now, my wife really will be most fearfully disappointed if you don't stay for tea. And so shall I!"

"In that case, I'd love to stay for tea, sir."

"Grand. That's grand." The Rector rose and ushered Adam back into the front parlour where a fire crackled and flames leapt in the hearth.

In the next room there was a new sound. The voices of young children at play.

The Rector's wife hobbled unsteadily out of the kitchen.

"Oh, there you are! I do hope my husband hasn't been bullying you, Wing-Commander?"

"I don't think the Wing-Commander lets anybody bully him, Adelaide." Eleanor Grafton said, emerging from the doorway, following the old lady into the hallway. She looked up as she stepped out of the shadows, and smiled sweetly as she met Adam's eye. "Not from what I've heard."

The last of Adam's dark thoughts fled. He grinned like an idiot.

"Why, hello, again."

Adelaide rounded on Eleanor.

"Ellie! You've already met the Wing-Commander! Why ever didn't you say, dear?"

Eleanor laughed.

"Actually, we've met twice."

"Twice?"

"Once when we were waiting for a train that was late," Adam explained. "And then the other day in the woods."

The Reverend Naismith-Parry and his wife exchanged glances, eyes widening knowingly. The Rector could not help but be struck by how effortlessly Eleanor had brought the young tyro's defences crashing down. For her part his wife noted that Eleanor, normally so cool and so reserved, was positively aglow in the Wing-Commander's presence.

It seemed Ellie had made a conquest.

The adults settled in chairs around the blazing fire. The conversation flowed around and mostly past Adam who was happy to sit and listen, limiting himself to the odd well-intentioned monosyllable, when pressed. Every time he looked up he seemed to find Eleanor's face. She was as intent on reading his thoughts as he was on reading hers. Adelaide Naismith-Parry monopolized the affair.

"I really don't know what I'd do without Ellie, Wing-Commander. She's an angel. I don't get around as well as I'd like, these days. And Ellie's always helping out. Here in the Rectory, and all around the parish. There's always so much to be done, you see." Adelaide tended to get carried away with the sound of her own voice, and to wander unwittingly into a world of her own. Her prattle was harmless, unconscious. Her husband watched over her. "Of course, the village has never been the same since the Royal Air Force came. Standards aren't what they used to be. Are they, Simon?"

"Sometimes, my love, I wonder if standards were ever

what they used to be," the Rector countered, ruefully. Later, when he mentioned the forthcoming funeral of Q-Queenie's bomb-aimer his wife threw up her hands in horror.

"Oh, the poor boy!"

The clock on the mantelpiece ticked loudly. The Rector sucked on his pipe.

"It must be strange coming to Ansham Wolds?" He posed, disappearing behind a cloud of fragrant, Virginia tobacco smoke. "Taking over the reins from a friend. Wing-Commander Fulshawe spoke of you more than once. You were together on Wellingtons when the balloon went up, I gather?"

"Yes, sir," Adam grimaced, tried not to fidget or draw attention to his unease. "We had our fair share of er, spills."

"I can imagine. Bert told me you're a fluent German speaker?"

"*Ich furchte, dass mein Deutsch rostig mit missbrauch von spät gewachsen ist,*" Adam responded, mischievously.

The Rector opened his mouth to reply, then not knowing what to say, shut it.

"*I fear my German has grown rusty with misuse of late,*" Adam explained, apologetically. "Bert encouraged me to keep it up. He said it would come in handy when I got shot down."

"Oh."

"How on earth did you learn to speak German?" Eleanor interjected.

"My mother's people were from Frankfurt and my father had extensive business interests in Germany. When I was a boy we went to Germany every summer. In Germany I'd speak German, and when my German friends came over to England, they'd speak English. We all took it for granted. You do when you're little, I suppose."

Eleanor smiled but behind her smile there was a hint of sadness, a flicker of trouble in her brown eyes. The man saw it, noted it for future reference. He wondered at the depths in her, worried that he might inadvertently have said something wrong, wounding.

"Did you have many German friends?" She asked.

He nodded.

Eleanor thought about this.

"Do you think of them often?"

Again, he nodded.

In the background the Rector coughed, cleared his throat.

"This must be a difficult time for Bert's wife?"

Adam dragged his eyes away from Eleanor's face.

"Er, yes. I should imagine Helen will take the children to her parents. In Norfolk. Until she's got her bearings, again."

The Rector clasped his hands on his lap. "Bert once showed me a photograph of his wife. She was some years younger than him, I believe? A lovely woman. And such fine children. I wrote to her as soon as I heard the bad news. She sent me back a very pleasant note. She hadn't made up her mind at that time whether she would be travelling up here to visit Bert's grave. She sounds like a very sensible, level-headed girl?"

"Yes, sir. I've suggested that if Helen plans to come up, she should let me know so that I can make the necessary arrangements."

"Of course. Forgive me, I hope you don't think I'm interfering."

"Not at all." Adam unconsciously bit his lower lip. "It's not a thing I'd like to go beyond these walls, sir. But Bert was not himself in the days leading up to the, er, accident, and I've taken the view that this is probably best kept from Helen."

"Of course. If his wife corresponds with me again I shall be the soul of discretion."

"Thank you, sir."

Eleanor stared into the fire. She detected the subtext in the two men's conversation, something each man was reading between the lines. There was a horrid rumour going round the village that Wing-Commander Fulshawe had had some sort of a fit and gone berserk. Adam Chantrey's defensiveness gave new substance to the rumour.

"There has been a deal of unfortunate talk," the Rector sighed.

"Quite," Adam agreed.

Eleanor listened in silence. She had met Wing-Commander Fulshawe frequently at the Rectory, where he was a regular visitor and sometimes after Evensong, at which he sang lustily from the body of the congregation. Once, in the week before his death she had passed him walking in the woods. He had hardly looked up when she called to him, grunted a reply, and brusquely stalked on into the trees. She had smelled drink on his breath. The poor man. He was lucky to have friends like Adam Chantrey to guard his good name.

The children amused themselves heedless of the adults.

"Can I give you a lift down the hill." Adam suggested to Eleanor when evening had drawn in and it was time to go.

"It's not on the way back to the airfield," she warned him, collecting her offspring and their coats.

"Detail," he grinned. "Besides, it's about to rain again. Quite hard, I shouldn't wonder." The woman looked at him, thoughtful for a moment. She gave in. Bidding farewells to their hosts they walked to the lane. The air was damp, freshly chilled.

"What a lovely old car," Eleanor said happily when they were alone with the children. It was the same car her brother had mentioned so many times in his letters, the car the 'Boscombe boys' had 'inherited' and brought with them to Kelmington when Adam had taken command of 380 Squadron. The car Dave, Bill Simmons, the New Zealand sheep farmer, and Max Reville the former Oxford rugby blue had used as their personal taxi to the drinking holes of Lincoln. Except, that was, when 'the Wingco pulled rank' and disappeared off to visit 'this week's mystery woman'. In recent days Eleanor had re-read her brother's letters, each and every one. Re-read them with a new, keen attentiveness to both detail and nuance. "Do you think we'll all fit in?"

"We'll soon see."

Jonathan made himself comfortable in the narrow space behind the seats and Emily sat sleepily on her mother's lap. Adam smiled at the girl, then Eleanor. The darkness now hung about them like a shield. As the car rolled down the lane a fine drizzle misted the windscreen.

"You said it would rain," the woman murmured.

Adam peered into the gloom. The lane ran between high hedgerows. The road was rutted and slippery with mud recently washed off the verges.

"We live just around the next bend," Eleanor told him, presently. "In the old Gatekeeper's Lodge."

Adam swung the Bentley off the lane, through the gateway and parked up close to the darkened cottage. Cutting the motor he clambered out, moved round the bonnet and opened the passenger door. Emily yawned as she was handed to the ground. Without thinking the man swept the child up in his arms.

"Tired, eh?" He whispered. The girl smiled shyly at him.

Eleanor stepped out, watching them. The rain fell harder.

"Wing-Commander Fulshawe has a daughter of Emmy's age?" She asked, very softly. "Does Emmy remind you of her?"

The man shook his head.

"No, it's not that. Katie's not quite three."

"Then what?"

Adam met her gaze.

"I suppose she reminds me of what it's like to be normal," he said, unable to completely mask his weariness.

They looked at each other for a moment.

"Will you come in for a cup of tea?" Eleanor asked.

He hesitated, knowing the time had come for him to politely say good night and to be on his way. He preached single-minded application to ops to his crews, railed against distractions or diversions from the deadly work of flying, fighting and surviving. He tried hard to pretend that personal attachments were luxuries a man in his position must shun. And then Eleanor had walked onto the platform of Thurlby Station. She had been in his thoughts ever since.

"If I may," he muttered.

Eleanor went inside to draw the blackout curtains while he waited in the porch, Emily in his arms. "I wonder where father is?" The woman asked out aloud as she shut the front door and lit a lamp. The mystery was soon resolved. Laughing ruefully, she showed Adam the scrawled note that had been waiting for her on the oaken sideboard.

Adam lowered Emily to the ground.

Dear Ellie,

I've been called back to London. Something's come up. They've sent a car for me. Don't go worrying your pretty head about me. I'm feeling much restored - quite spoiled, actually.

Bit of a shame getting called back to town before I got around to paying my respects to Alex and his new Squadron Commander. Never mind, there will be other opportunities, no doubt.

Say good bye to Johnny and Emmy for me.
All my love,
Father.

"The Prof's off on his travels again, then," Adam said, mightily relieved.

"The Prof?" Eleanor queried, picking up not so much on what the man had said, but the tone in which it he had said it. Respect inter-mingled with a touch of irony.

"Ah," Adam sighed. He had assumed that she knew, more or less, where her father sat in the Air Ministry and moreover, had some general idea of the work on which he was engaged. Her tone suggested otherwise. "Our paths have crossed, as it were."

"Oh, I see." Eleanor replied, none the wiser.

Adam pulled off his cap.

"Look, before we go any further," he said, taking the bull by the horns. "I think it is only fair that I tell you the Prof and I don't exactly get on."

Eleanor was intrigued, now. Really intrigued.

"My father keeps his cards close to his chest. He never talks about his work. I only know what little Dave told me. So, Father doesn't approve of you?"

"No, not at all. Sorry."

Eleanor laughed. She could not help herself.

"Are you sure?"

"Oh, yes," Adam confirmed, perplexed by her gaiety. "When a chap goes out of his way to get you cashiered I usually take it as a sign that he doesn't approve of one. I always have in the past, anyway."

Eleanor laughed, again. For a moment she wondered if he was teasing her but discounted the notion almost immediately.

He was viewing her intently.

"Is it likely to be a problem?"

The question sobered Eleanor. "No, of course not." She started to take off her coat and he helped her disentangle her arms from the sleeves. "When I told Father I'd met you at the station he didn't mention anything about wanting you cashiered?"

She took the man's cap and laid it on the sideboard.

"It's all ancient history. I'm not a great one for raking over ancient history," he continued, hastily. "It doesn't do anybody any good."

Eleanor bent down to pick up the children's coats. "Father brightened up no end when I told him you might be calling in to pay your respects. Do you remember? You promised? When you rescued me in the woods the other day?"

"Things have been a bit hectic, lately." Adam apologized, following her deeper into the cottage. It was chilly and she busied herself with setting the fire in the grate, raking away the cold, dead ashes.

"Can I do anything?"

"No, it's all right."

He fidgeted as she knelt by the hearth.

"Do sit down," she chided. "You're making me nervous."

Adam did as he was told.

He sat down, glanced around the room. After years wandering from one impersonal, Spartan billet to another he was struck by the homeliness of his surroundings. It was a long time since he had had a home. Home was a strange, half-remembered idea. On the squadrons nobody put down roots: there was no future in it. Surviving meant another posting, a call to somewhere new and different, somewhere miles from anywhere, godforsaken and as lonely as the last place.

Eleanor left him as flames flickered in the grate, smiled at him as she walked through into the kitchen. He listened to her moving around. Waiting for her to return he stirred life into the fire, placed more log chips from the small, neat stack beside the hearth into the flames. The fire was blazing when Eleanor re-appeared bearing a tray.

"I should have left the fire in your hands in the first place, Wing-Commander," she observed, putting down the tea things.

"I'm afraid the fires I light often tend to get a bit out of hand."

Eleanor giggled, despite herself. It was a horrible thing to say and yet so boyish that she could not help but see the funny side of it. She sat in the armchair opposite him.

"You were very quiet this afternoon?"

"Sorry, I didn't have that much to say."

"We seem to keep bumping into each other, don't we?"

He scratched his chin.

"I wonder what it all means?"

The question triggered alarm bells. Things were happening too fast and Eleanor needed a little breathing space, a pause for thought. She attempted to make polite conversation.

"Simon and Wing-Commander Fulshawe were on very good terms. Sometimes, Simon can be a little over-powering. You mustn't be too hard on him."

"He told me about his son," the man said, shrugging. "Oh, and about forgiveness." This bewildered the woman. The man lifted a hand, grinned. "We agreed to differ."

Eleanor sipped her tea.

"Sorry," he went on. "I'm not very good company."

"Oh, I wouldn't say that!" Eleanor objected, instantly. Adam Chantrey was easily the most interesting man she had met since she could hardly remember when. Moreover, she was in imminent danger of being utterly...captivated by him.

"You'll be wanting to put the children to bed," Adam thought out aloud. "You mustn't let me get under you feet."

Eleanor took him at his word and went off to organize her youngsters. It was some time later, the best part of half-an-hour, when she brought the boy and the girl into the front room to say good night to the famous Wing-Commander. They discovered their guest dozing by the fire, deaf to the world. Another twenty minutes elapsed before Eleanor finally returned to give him her full attention. He blinked awake as she entered the room.

"I've made more tea."

He rubbed his eyes.

"Capital." They were truly alone for the first time. Adam gestured at the photographs framed on the mantelpiece above the hearth. Wedding portraits, prints of the children, several of the family, mother, father and toddlers, and a pair of pictures snapped at Boscombe Down the previous year. "Your husband?" He asked, indicating the photograph of a slim man in subaltern's dress.

"Just before he went overseas." Eleanor poured the tea. "You never explained how you knew it was going to rain?" The room was dim and warm, and the flames in the hearth cast shadows at their backs.

"Oh, that. I get all the latest meteorological forecasts."

"Oh, that's cheating!"

"Absolutely."

"You're the talk of the village," she prompted, gently teasing him out of his shell.

"You mustn't believe everything you hear."

"And do you think I do?"

"No."

"No," she echoed. "You're not at all what I expected, actually?"

From habit Adam dug out his cigarette case, retrieved a cigarette.

"Only the one head, you mean? Sorry, do you mind

if I smoke?"

"No, not at all."

He struck a match, flicked the spent light into the fire.

"I hope you're not making fun of me, Wing-Commander?" Eleanor asked, momentarily unable to drag her eyes off him.

"Wouldn't dream of it."

"You do say the most peculiar things." A quietness fell between them as they searched for their lost thoughts in the lap and flicker of the flames that warmed their faces. "But I don't mind. That's the oddest thing."

Sitting with him in the stillness of the cottage Eleanor was at peace with herself and her world. She understood what she was doing. Her eyes were wide open. Involvement with this man was a terrible risk but she did not care. Adam regarded her with eyes that betrayed his misgivings as if he had realised, intuitively, that she had already made her decisions and that whatever would be would be. She met his gaze unafraid.

"It's funny," she sighed, "but seeing you with Emmy, I just couldn't imagine you doing the things they say you've done?"

"I hope I'm not a disappointment?"

"No," she smiled. "You're not a disappointment. In fact, if I'm not very, very careful I shall become quite besotted with you." It was said in a guilty rush. Doubts assailed her. Suddenly, she was afraid she was making a fool of herself with a complete, younger stranger. It was absurd, she hardly knew him or he her.

Adam saw it all in her hazel brown eyes.

"I have a confession of my own," he returned, trying to stay calm, in control. "I think I was smitten waiting for a certain train that was late."

"We're not being silly?"

He shook his head.

"No, I don't think so."

"But we're strangers?"

"Everybody is to begin with."

They looked to each other for courage.

"I'd best be making tracks," he said in a voice that was not his own.

"Of course." Eleanor wanted him to stay.

They walked together to the door where they paused in the darkness.

"I don't suppose there's any point asking you to take care?" She inquired, trying to sound cheerful.

"I'm supposed to be the crazy new Wingco, remember?"

"Be careful, anyway? For me?"

"For you, then."

The rain was tumbling from the sky.

"When will I see you again?" She regretted saying it even as the words spilled from her lips.

"I don't know. Soon I hope."

She moved close to him, put her arms around his neck and drew his mouth down to hers. He wrapped her in his embrace, drew her against him. They kissed, tentatively at first, then slowly, intimately.

Eleanor waved into the blackness as the Bentley drove off into the falling rain. She was trembling as she shut the door. The sensation of his mouth on hers, the presence of him, the strong circle of his arms holding her tight lingered as if he was still in the room. Only he was not. He was gone and she might never see him again. Every time they said good bye it might be for the last time.

Her ordered, sane little world had just turned upside down.

Chapter 13

Tuesday 12th October, 1943
St. Paul's Church, Ansham Wolds, Lincolnshire

Flight Sergeant William O'Hara's coffin rested on the beams above the open grave.

The north-east corner of the churchyard was given over to the dead of Bomber Command. Nineteen crosses marked the final resting places of 647 Squadron's fallen, another thirteen the graves of men of other squadrons who had died attempting to land their crippled aircraft at Ansham Wolds.

The crews of Ewan McDonald's A Flight had trooped down to the village *en masse*, filled the small, hilltop church. Group Captain Alexander was flanked by Adam and Mac, aircrew stood several ranks deep behind them. Opposite were a score of villagers, the majority women. The licensee of the hamlet's solitary Public House, the Sherwood Arms, Arnold Bowman and his wife Betty, stood together a little apart from their neighbours. Eleanor, having shepherded Adelaide Naismith-Parry to her pew inside the church, now guided the old lady across the wet grass to take her place among her husband's parishioners.

The Rector coughed to clear his throat. The rain had held off but overhead the clouds rolled east, threatening an imminent downpour.

"Man that is born of woman hath but a short time to live, and is full of misery. He cometh up, and is cut down, like a flower; he fleeth as it were a shadow, and never continueth in one stay..."

Bomber Command's dead were usually buried far away, seen off by strangers and aircrew rarely witnessed the horrors wrought on the bodies of their comrades. The battle could seem faraway, a little unreal because unlike infantrymen, aircrew fought their war at arm's length.   They watched other aircraft going down, burning, tumbling, and disintegrating in the night. Aircrew casualties tended to be anonymous, faceless.

"In the midst of life we are in death: of whom may we seek for succour, but of thee, O Lord, who for our sins art justly displeased..."

Q-Queenie's bomb-aimer had not died in vain. The Pathfinders had discovered clear skies over Hanover and laid a tight carpet of red ground markers in the heart of the city. The subsequent bombing had been unusually concentrated despite the arrival of a large number of night fighters while the attack was still in full swing. Indications were that the main bombing effort had crept back less than two miles, never reaching open country and that the weight of the attack had fallen on built-up areas of the city. Reconnaissance photographs taken by a high-flying Mosquito thirty-six hours after the raid showed Hanover hidden beneath a huge pall of smoke.

"Yet, O Lord God most holy, O Lord most mighty, O holy and most merciful Saviour, deliver us not into the bitter pains of eternal death..."

Adam looked to his front, every now and then stealing a glance towards Eleanor. He could not help himself. He bowed his head, stared at the flag draped over the coffin.

"Thou knowest, Lord, the secrets of our hearts; shut not thy merciful ears to our prayer; but spare us, Lord most holy, O God most mighty, O holy and merciful Saviour, thou most worthy judge eternal, suffer us not, at our last hour, for any pains of death, to fall from thee..."

The wind was picking up from the south-west. It gusted across the churchyard, plucked at coat tails, chilled exposed skin and watered eyes. Coinciding with the full moon period Atlantic gales were pushing a succession of storm fronts across northern Europe, forcing a lull in the battle. The weather had grounded the Main Force and made a mockery of 647 Squadron's training schedule. Until the intervention of the weather Group had been growing restive about the large number of hours his crews were flying. Fuel for training, and other non-operational duties was limited, strictly rationed, each Squadron's variable allocation fixed month by month. The Supply Staff at Bawtry Hall had concluded that 647 Squadron was being 'recklessly' profligate with its allocation, and formally cautioned 'the Officer Commanding' that if he 'continued to exceed authorized 100-octane allocation levels' he could expect to be summoned to Bawtry Hall to account for his actions. The memo also informed him that the AOC had been notified of the 'present unsatisfactory situation'. That was just before the weather had curbed the Squadron's 'reckless profligacy'.

Adam had written a terse memo to the Group Supply Officer, copied to the AOC, inquiring precisely how he was expected to 'ensure the operational readiness of my crews without consuming 100-octane?' That very morning 647 Squadron's Supply Officer had been despatched to Bawtry Hall bearing the incendiary missive and ordered to 'bring back Group's written response.' He knew he was stirring up a hornet's nest and in due course, he fully expected to be sternly reprimanded. No matter. If the AOC asked him to explain himself he would be more than happy to oblige him. If old lags like him did not speak up for their crews what use were they?

Flight Sergeant William O'Hara's coffin was slowly lowered into the grave. The Reverend Naismith-Parry stooped stiffly to grasp a handful of dry earth from beneath one corner of the tarpaulin that had kept the rain off the freshly dug earth.

"Forasmuch as it hath pleased Almighty God of his great mercy to take unto himself the soul of our dear brother here departed, we therefore commit his body to the ground; earth to earth, ashes to ashes, dust to dust;

in sure and certain hope of the Resurrection to eternal life, through our Lord Jesus Christ; who shall change our vile body, that it may be like unto his glorious body, according to the mighty working, whereby he is able to subdue all things to himself..."

"Our Father, which art in heaven, Hallowed be thy name..." The crews spontaneously picked up the words of the Lord's Prayer. They spoke as one man. "Thy kingdom come. Thy will be done, in earth as it is in heaven. Give us this day our daily bread. And forgive us our trespasses. As we forgive them that trespass against us. And lead us not into temptation; but deliver us from evil..."

Adam said the words silently to himself, humbled. A volley of shots was fired over the grave. Later, as the crews marched down the hill to the buses waiting to take them back to the airfield, he thanked each of the villagers who had attended the funeral service.

"Least we could do," said Betty Bowman. "Fine lads, every one of them!" She declared defiantly.

"Here! Here!" Seconded her husband, a rotund man with John Bull mutton chop whiskers and a red face.

His duty done Adam approached Eleanor.

"The boy had no family except the Squadron," he said. He had not seen her since Saturday night. It went without saying that he had a thousand and one things to do at the station, and that he had been infernally busy. Notwithstanding, he could and should have made time to see her again, and to speak to her. A brief visit to the cottage, a note of some kind, anything to renew contact. He shrugged, feeling awkward, guilty. "It was good of you to come."

"Do you have to go back straight away?" She asked. Adelaide Naismith-Parry was talking animatedly with her husband and Group Captain Alexander as they guided her patiently along the path to the Rectory.

"No," he muttered.

The first big, heavy drops of rain splashed on the brim of his cap. In seconds the deluge was upon them, the water falling from the heavens in a curtain. The man and the woman stared at each other, she seized his hand and led him across the sodden turf to the sanctuary of the vaulted porch over the main door of the church. They ran into the dry as the downpour hammered on the roof.

"Oh, dear," she gasped. "I hope Simon and Adelaide don't get too wet."

"Won't they wonder where you've got to?"

"No, I don't think so," she replied, her brown eyes twinkling. "They'll assume I'm with you."

"Oh, I see."

The brief squall was passing over. The man tore his gaze from her face, stared out across the valley, its verdant slopes, scattered houses, its greenery as yet barely faded with the onset of autumn.

"Simon and Adelaide will be expecting me at the Rectory," she prompted, gently. "Will you join me?"

"I'd like to," he shrugged. "I ought to be getting back, though."

Eleanor accepted this without demur.

"Will you let me cook you dinner one night this week?"

He looked into her eyes. "When did you think?"

"Thursday. About seven?"

"I shall look forward to it."

"Good. It's a date, then." she smiled.

"Until Thursday, then."

Eleanor smiled, pressed his hands.

"Now, off you go!"

There was no parting kiss this afternoon. The man turned and was gone, hurrying into the post-squall drizzle.

Helen Fulshawe's letter was waiting for Adam when he got back to the station. He recognised her handwriting on the envelope.

Rose Cottage,
Moorehampstead, Gloucestershire
4th October

Dearest Adam,

Like you, I had come to believe that Bert was indestructible. But of course, he wasn't. He just behaved as if he was. But that was Bert and if he had been any different, he wouldn't have been the lovely, brave, kind man I married.

Thank you for trying to protect me. I think I know what probably happened. What really happened, that is. Thank you for trying to protect me.

I miss him terribly.

I hope you won't be offended (or think me a complete hypocrite) but despite everything, Bert was always the centre of my world. He was from the beginning. I always loved him. Really, truly. Not the way I ought to have loved him, but I did love him. You see, whatever happened, I knew he'd always have me back. Whoever I'd been with and whatever I'd done he would always have me back and he wouldn't dream of making any kind of scene about it.

I've tried so hard not to think what I'd do if and when this day came that I don't really know what to make of things. I don't know what I'd do if it wasn't for the children. One has to keep up appearances for them, even though I'm sure they see straight through it.

I know you must miss Bert as I do. Nobody in the world was closer to him than you. I used to be so jealous. It is ridiculous, I know, but I used to resent the fact that Bert never had any secrets from you. Forgive me if this sounds a little odd but you two were more than brothers. It was because you'd been through so much together, I suppose. Bert said that if Jack grew up to be like you, he would die a happy man. I know you don't have much time for such sentimental gushings, but there it is. I've said it now, and I feel better for it!

When I get over Bert's death, and sooner or later I will start to get over it, I mean to make a new life for myself and the children. I've seen too many of my friends give up. I shall never give in. Bert wouldn't have wanted me to spend the rest of my life in black. I shall grieve for Bert, but then I shall get on with things. The children are all that matters. Bert's gone, but I still have the children.

I know you will feel responsible. That you will want to help and want to do the "right thing". However, you must not feel responsible. You have your life to live, and your war to fight. You are not like Bert. Bert was a throwback. If he'd been at Balaklava he'd have been on the first horse charging down the Valley of Death. Probably laughing into the muzzles of the Russian guns! Bert was never meant to survive. How he survived two tours I shall never know. He always said you could fly rings around him blindfolded, that you were one of those chaps who might one day fly a hundred ops. Bert was a purebred warrior, everything he did was in anger with his blood well and truly up. It is different for you. If you put your mind to it you might just come through this whole dreadful business in one piece.

If you are to get through it, you can't afford to be worrying about me or the children. Or about *what might have been. Especially, not about what Bert would have thought if he'd known about us.*

You will always be my dearest friend, Adam. Always. I regret being unfaithful to Bert, the lies and the deceptions. I regret many things. But I'm not ashamed of what we did. Or of anything I've done. And neither should you be. Blame it on the war. I was in love with two men, either of you, both of you could have been taken from me at any time. Gone in a single night, lost forever and I couldn't bear the thought of that so I clung to you both. In the beginning you were like the two opposite sides of the same coin, Bert was loud and brash and clumsy, you were so calm and collected and I allowed things to go too far. I say this now because you must not be guilty about it. It happened. You weren't to blame, I could have stopped it happening if I'd wanted but the truth is that I wanted it to happen.

Anyway, you must get on with things. Whatever lies ahead, you and I must travel our own roads. I plan to take the children to my parents. We shall not want for anything. My father, as you know, farms and has a finger in lots of pies in the City (yes, I know you think he's a war profiteer, most likely, he is), but he's a dear old stick at heart and I'm still the apple of his eye, and I know mother will be a brick. Things will be easier once we've moved back to Norfolk. You may think going back to Faldwell is a mistake (memories and so forth). Well, it will only be until I decide what to do next. I must get away from Rose Cottage because until I do I cannot make a new start. And I do have to make a new start.

Please don't think I'm being selfish. I can't live with memories. Not just memories. When the sky falls you have to make a new start, a new beginning. Otherwise you end up living in the past and our pasts are far too painful for that. Jack and Kate must learn to look to the future, not backwards. It is up to me to set them the right example.

So, dearest Adam, remember Bert as fondly as I always will but let him go, let him rest in peace. Try not to be too hard on him for going out the way he did. I'm sure you will do a fine job at Ansham Wolds. I'm glad it is you taking over from Bert.

Take good care of yourself or I shall never, ever forgive you. You owe it to Bert, to me, to all those poor fellows who died on the way back from Wilhelmshaven, and to all the others we have known who have died since to survive. Somebody must survive, otherwise who will tell our children what happened and why? And why it must never be allowed to happen again. Isn't that what all this is supposed to be about? The war? The killing? The unspeakable things we are doing to places like Hamburg and Cologne? If we ever let it happen again it will all have been for nothing, and that would be obscene. I can't bear the thought of that. I don't think you can, either.

So, dearest Adam, take care.
All my love,
Helen.

Chapter 14

Peter Tilliard sat in the cab of the Bedford lorry maintaining a weary watchful eye on the erks hauling G-George into position. All that day A Flight's Lancaster's had been re-aligning their .303 Browning machine guns. It was a laborious process involving each aircraft being towed over to the far side of the airfield, and lined up with the gun butts for live firing trials.

"Char's up, sir," announced the weather-beaten duty flight sergeant fitter, clambering wearily up into the cab.

"Thanks, Chiefy," Tilliard said, taking the proffered mug. "We'll be out here for hours yet at this rate."

"Yes, sir."

The younger man lapsed into contemplation. Nobody had questioned the alignment of the squadron's guns before now. The accepted wisdom was that rounds fired from the Brownings mounted in the turrets of the Squadron's Lancasters should converge at a range of three hundred yards.

Not according to the new Wingco.

'Frankly, there's not a lot of point aligning your guns to three hundred yards,' Chantrey had remarked to his Flight Commanders. 'I don't care how many carrots *our* gunners eat, they aren't going to see a fighter until it's a bloody sight closer than that. And anyway, even if they do spot a fighter at that sort of range the last thing you want them to do is open fire and give away the position of your aircraft. *My* gunners align to a hundred yards.'

It was a small thing, a detail. Mac had thought about it, taken soundings among his senior crews. Pointedly, the Wingco had not issued a standing order dictating compliance with his advice. He had left the decision with his Flight Commanders. While B Flight had no plans to re-align its guns, Mac had decided that his flight would re-align as soon as possible. He had ordered Peter Tilliard to 'see to it'.

"The range is clear, sir."

"Carry on, Chiefy." Thirty yards away the four Brownings in the rear-turret opened up. A stream of bullets ripped into the butts, churning wet earth. Spent cartridge cases spilled out of the back of the turret, clattering onto the wet tarmac, rolling into heaps. Mac's insistence that the re-alignments be checked by extended live-firing tests, had as anticipated, exposed numerous faults in the turrets of A Flight's aircraft.

The Chief's book was rapidly filling with notes.

'Do you really think it'll make any difference, Mac?' Tilliard had asked his Flight Commander, initially unconvinced.

'Maybe. Anything that evens up the odds a bit is worth trying, don't you think?'

'I suppose it won't do any harm,' he had agreed. The problem was that ever since Mac had detailed him to 'make sure that the job's done properly', he had had precious little opportunity to renew acquaintance with Suzy.

The twin Brownings of G-George's Fraser Nash type 50 mid-upper turret opened fire. Briefly.

Jammed!

"Third jam today, Chiefy," Tilliard observed, scowling. "Bloody good thing we're not operating tonight!"

"Yes, sir." The notations in the NCO's book became more feverish.

Tilliard was thoroughly unamused by the day's work. The failure rate was alarmingly high and he wanted to know why. Mac knew he would follow up on each and every problem. His friend had almost certainly worked out by now that it had been Suzy with him outside *The Liberty*; this whole exercise might simply be Mac's way of keeping him from seeing Suzy and saving him from himself.

"Give a dog a bone and he'll shake it," Tilliard said to himself.

Tilliard understood how it was that Mac had hit it off with the new Wingco while the ebullient, dashing Barney Knight had suddenly developed a bad case of two left feet. The CO was a strange cove, every bit as press on as Bert Fulshawe and in his own way as fanatically intolerant of failure. The difference was that whereas Fulshawe had regarded operations as an end in themselves; Chantrey made little or no distinction between training and ops. Under Bert Fulshawe's regime the Squadron had gone to war every third or fourth night, under the new Wingco, 647 Squadron was at war *every day and every night*. Bert Fulshawe had *talked* a good war; his successor was wholly focussed on *fighting* a good war.

Mac was cast in a similar mould to the Wingco, albeit a somewhat diffident incarnation. His friend lacked the Wingco's lightness of touch with the crews but Tilliard had seen the change in him of late, and the new spring in his step. Mac was a fast learner and beneath the stoic exterior, shrewd, nobody's fool. There was a knock on the door of the Bedford's cab.

Initially, Tilliard was a little peeved to have his thoughts so rudely perturbed.

"Could *we* have a word, sir?"

Tilliard leaned out of the window, looked down. Recognising the Wingco's flight engineer, Flying Officer Ted Hallowes, his half-scowl softened. The other man squinted up at him, a cigarette shielded against the wind in his cupped right hand.

"Private, like, sir?"

Tilliard blinked.

"All right, Ted," he agreed, curious. "Keep an eye on things, Chiefy. I won't be long." He clambered down, followed Hallowes around to the back of the lorry where four other men were waiting, all smoking. Five members of the Wingco's crew closed about him. Only Ben Hardiman was absent.

It seemed Ted Hallowes was the nominated spokesman.

"It's like this," he began, without ado. "The Wingco's going to fly one in three ops from now on. Tops. That leaves us sitting on our hands most nights. Not good. Too much time to think. You know the drill. Word is you're looking for a crew?"

Momentarily, Tilliard was too stunned to speak. He had resigned himself to the prospect of flying with sprogs when he eventually got back on ops.

"Why, yes."

"Right," Ted Hallowes declared, taking a drag on his cigarette. "Next couple of ops you do, we'll tag along. If that's okay?"

Tilliard was tempted to pinch himself. Once it got around that the Wingco's crew had volunteered to fly with him every unassigned old lag in 1 Group would be hammering on his door. He struggled to pull himself together.

"Are you chaps absolutely sure about this?"

The circle of heads nodded. Hallowes ground the butt of his cigarette underfoot.

"It's like this. If we had the choice we'd fly all our ops with the Wingco because he's the best. No argument. Trouble is flying with the Wingco we're going to be flying this bloody tour for ever. The way we look at it you're the next best Lancaster driver in these parts. So we'll fly a couple of ops with you. Keep our hands in, like."

"Have you cleared this with Wing-Commander Chantrey?"

"Nope, that's your job, Skipper," this from a broken-nosed, grinning Taffy Davies.

Hallowes shoved his hands in his greatcoat pockets.

"We'll need a decent nav. Nothing personal but the Nav Leader only flies with the Wingco. No exceptions. So count him out, like."

"Any ideas?" Tilliard inquired, in a daze now.

"Forget about sprogs," Hallowes said, thinking out aloud. "We'll put out the word. There's one or two old lags hanging around without a regular berth."

"There's that Aussie, Jack Gordon?" Suggested Bert Pound, thoughtfully. "He seems a good sort. Second tour man. He won't want to go flying with sprogs if he can help it?"

"Right, I'll have a word," Hallowes agreed. "If not him, I'm sure we'll find somebody who fits the bill."

Tilliard's head was spinning. He was beaming like an idiot and he knew it. He did not care, not one jot.

"Right, ho."

"That's settled, then!"

Hands were shaken and the contract agreed.

Chapter 15

Thursday 14th October, 1943
RAF Ansham Wolds, Lincolnshire

Yesterday had been Barney Knight's twenty-third birthday and B Flight had celebrated in style. Adam awoke feeling more than a little worse for wear. Helen's letter had shaken him, probed old and painful scar tissue. He brooded, tried to convince himself that Helen was right. That the past was the past and there was no going back, that there was no point in wishing things were otherwise. In the end he had let down his guard and allowed himself to get drunk.

At the height of the proceedings somebody, probably Ben, had prevailed on him to take a turn at the piano. He recollected joining in the bawdy chorus and this morning his hoarse voice and sore throat bore testimony to the event. Thankfully, the forecast of more storms and the rising Moon ruled out operations that night. After most *Mess Nights* a morning constitutional across the aerodrome with Rufus was sufficient to blow away the cobwebs. Not so this morning; he had admitted defeat and allowed Group Captain Alexander's blond WAAF driver to walk the dog.

When, later that morning and still a little thick-headed, he stuck his head around the Station Master's door – which, to the Old Man's credit was invariably open - he was unpleasantly surprised to discover the Senior WAAF in residence. Group Captain Alexander was the sort of Station Master who enjoyed a chinwag mid-morning, the chance to have a relaxed, confidential chat with his Squadron Commander over a cup of tea. He was *not* the sort of Station Master who liked the brief, precious tranquillity of his mid-mornings rudely compromised by what he considered peripheral 'non-operational matters'. It was readily apparent from his strained expression that the Old Man's mid-morning repose had been sorely interrupted by his unwanted visitor and that for all his old world civility he was not amused. Adam stifled a groan and entered the room. Squadron Officer Laing was not a woman to be trifled with at the best of times and from the positively Churchillian set of her features, he deduced that today she had donned her witch finder general's hat.

"Ah, there you are," Group Captain Alexander frowned. "Take a pew. Perhaps," he went on, gruffly, to the Senior WAAF, "it would be best if you explained your, er, concerns, directly to Wing-Commander Chantrey?"

"Thank you, sir." The woman turned, fixed the younger man in her stare. Calmly, unhurriedly she sized up her quarry. Adam had yet to cross swords with the Senior WAAF. However, it seemed the evil moment could be delayed no longer. Allegedly, the woman was a dragon, a veritable battleaxe who guarded the well-being of 'her girls' - both physical and moral - with a deadly, indomitable and utterly humourless zeal.

Adam smiled amiably. That usually did the trick. Not today. The woman glowered back at him.

"The time has come when urgent action is imperative!" Squadron Officer Laing declared, loudly.

"Quite," murmured the Group Captain.

"Absolutely," Adam agreed. The next moment he reconsidered. "Er, sorry, what exactly are we talking about?"

This infuriated the Senior WAAF.

"I'm talking about the relations between some of your men, Wing-Commander, and my girls!"

"Oh, I see."

"And something must be done about it!"

Adam's head throbbed, unmercifully. He glanced at Group Captain Alexander who was busily packing his pipe. Confronted by a regiment of panzers the Old Man would have stood his ground and fought like a lion, roaring indefatigable defiance. Faced with an enraged Senior WAAF, he was keeping his head down below the parapet.

"I raised this matter," Squadron Officer Laing continued, "with Wing-Commander Fulshawe shortly before his unfortunate *accident*. He was most supportive. Most supportive. I trust that I can depend on your whole-hearted support in this matter?"

The woman was getting on Adam's nerves. Remembering that somebody had mentioned she abhorred smoking, he dug out a cigarette from Helen's silver case. Slowly, deliberately. Simultaneously, the Station Master struck a match, sucked on the stem of his pipe and began to waft clouds of sweet-smelling smoke around himself. Great minds thinking alike. "A smoke screen," he said to himself. That was what was called for, a smoke screen.

"Do forgive me," he apologised, earnestly. "Perhaps, it's just me and I'm being awfully dense. But I'm still not clear exactly what this, er, problem is that we're supposed to be discussing?"

"Why, the excessive familiarity of a certain element among *your* crews and some of *my* girls, Wing-Commander! Goodness! Two of *my* girls have been posted since *your* arrival on grounds of, of... Pregnancy!" The Senior WAAF was clearly mortified the new Squadron Commander was unaware of the deplorable goings on at Ansham Wolds.

Adam meanwhile, struggled to keep a straight face.

"My word. Two girls. Since *my* arrival," he echoed, out aloud. It was very, very hard not to see the funny side of things. "I believe that in the tropics they put bromide in the chaps' tea," he offered, poker-faced. "Perhaps, I could have a word with the Flight Surgeon?"

The Senior WAAF's exasperation boiled over.

"I had hoped you would adopt a more mature attitude to the solution of what is, after all, a mutual problem, Wing-Commander. This is not a laughing matter!"

Adam sobered, bleakness touched his eyes. He was tired and hung over. The woman was trying his patience and wasting his time.

"No, of course not, Squadron Officer Laing," he replied, not bothering to conceal his irritation. "I don't doubt for a moment that dear old Bert was all in favour of a full scale campaign of moral renewal. That was the kind of chap Bert was, bless him. However, I'm not Bert and the crews are *my* crews now, *not* Bert's."

"But it is a question of discipline!" Objected the Senior WAAF. "Sir!"

"I agree," he retorted. With an effort he bit his tongue, stopped himself telling Squadron Officer Laing what he really thought about her one woman moral crusade. "However," he continued, in a parody of a conciliatory tone, "I'm bound to say that the majority of our people are young and a long way from home and most likely, more than a little homesick. Yes, you are right, it is a question of discipline and I'm the last man who would wish to tolerate, let alone condone laxity in these matters. Nevertheless, discipline is worthless if it is applied blindly. Discipline must be administered even-handedly, and in respect of the relations between the men and women on this Station, we must never allow ourselves to forget that what we are up against, is human nature."

Group Captain Alexander nodded his vehement assent to every word.

"Here, here," he grunted.

Adam carried on. "Believe *me* I am under no illusion that *my* aircrew are angels. They are anything but. They are young men, and with due deference to your gender, madam, one can hardly expect them to behave in any other way than one might reasonably expect young men anywhere to behave. Boys will, I fear, be boys." He ought to have left it there. Added, unkindly: "And, in case you've forgotten, there is actually a war going on."

"But I..."

The Senior WAAF's protest fell on deaf ears.

"You must of course, refer specific complaints about the conduct of *my* men to *me* personally," Adam said, brusquely. "I shall give any such cases my fullest attention. Pending operational considerations, of course. Where regulations have been infringed I will take a very severe view of matters." With which he sat back in his chair. "A very severe view. Pending, as I said, *operational considerations*." Once again, he knew he ought to have stopped there but added, with what for him was an uncharacteristically saturnine grimace: "Fighting the King's enemies, and so forth."

Squadron Officer Laing opened her mouth, shut it again a moment later, thinking better of it. The two men in the room could almost see the workings of her mind. The Wingco had stated his position, offered her a measure of support. Or at least she thought he had. To have pressed her case further at this time, would have been bad form. Possibly, insubordinate.

"I've prepared a report, sir," she announced, lamely.

"I'd be glad of the opportunity to read it, if I may," Adam responded, blankly. He studied his wristwatch. "Was there anything else?"

Group Captain Alexander dismissed both his visitors.

"I hope you don't think I'm making a fuss over nothing, sir?" The woman asked as she trailed Adam down the corridor.

"Not at all," he assured her, stopping at the door to the squadron office. "You'll let me have a copy of that report as soon as possible?"

He sought refuge in the Adjutant's den.

Tom Villiers was at his desk and he looked up. He made as if to rise to his feet before the younger man waved him down. The Adjutant of was a bulky, taciturn man who knew more about what went on at Ansham Wolds than any other man alive. Which was precisely why Adam had never previously even considered raising the fraught subject of fraternization with him.

"There's a school of thought which holds that she means well, sir," the Adjutant remarked, deadpan.

"The blasted woman says she's got a report, Tom!" Adam complained, pacing the small room. "About fraternization or some such? Goodness knows what I'll find in it!"

Despite his obvious irritation the Wingco had not asked him a specific question and Tom Villiers with a relieved sigh, recognised as much. The Senior WAAF's preoccupations - familiar if somewhat hoary old chestnuts - were well known to him. Although he could have quoted his CO chapter and verse on the topic, it was in his opinion best for all concerned to let sleeping dogs lie. He had pleaded with Harriet Laing, with whom he had always enjoyed the most cordial of professional relations, not to make a scene, and cautioned her in no uncertain terms that from *everything* he had heard and seen of him, she was wasting her time harrying the *new* Wingco. Adam Chantrey was *not* Bert Fulshawe, and frankly, anybody who thought he was, was a fool to themselves and riding for a very hard fall.

'Look,' he had implored Harriet Laing, with a sinking feeling. 'Please hold your fire. Don't go rushing in like a bull in a china shop. You won't get anywhere. Not with this fellow! This chap's not like Jack Grant, or even Bert Fulshawe. He's not old school. Whatever happens, this chap will always go out to bat for his crews. Always, Harriet. No matter how sticky it gets, he won't give an inch.'

When the Wingco read the offending 'report' Harriet's days at Ansham Wolds, already numbered, would probably be over. It was one thing to be a well-intentioned busybody, the object of harmless light relief. Another entirely to meddle in aircrew matters. He was very much afraid that she had completely misjudged her man.

"Bloody witch!" Adam murmured as he stepped across to the window. He scowled out into the grey October morning. "Blast her! What the Devil am I going find in this report of hers, Tom?"

Now that the question had been asked Tom Villiers hesitated.

"No names, no pack drill?" The Wingco added quickly.

"Other than the normal off station, er, associations, between men and women from this and other local stations," the Adjutant prefaced, his voice pitched low, "Squadron Officer Laing may have caught wind of the fact that, occasionally, one or another of her charges avail themselves of the, er, opportunity for an, er, unofficial ride on one of our Lancs, sir. I gather there is a certain cachet among her young ladies in membership of the, er..."

To Villiers surprise, not to say consternation, the younger man turned back from the window chuckling grimly.

"The *Lancaster Heaven Club*?" Adam inquired, digging out a cigarette.

"Quite, sir. How did you know?"

"Whatever the Senior WAAF may think, original sin wasn't invented at Ansham Wolds, Tom," Adam observed. He viewed the Adjutant thoughtfully for a moment. Shook his head. "I can't believe she's actually going through channels!"

"No, sir,"

"I take it as read that you've tried to talk her out of this damned fool 'report' nonsense?"

Tom Villiers was disconcerted to discover how far ahead of him the new Wingco was. The man had been at

Ansham Wolds less than three weeks and he seemed to have the whole place under his thumb.

"Yes, sir."

"Be a good fellow. Have another go. If you would, please."

"I'll do my best, sir." Villiers could not make himself sound optimistic about the outcome of a renewed intervention.

With which Adam moved on.

"Have we been officially stood down, yet?"

"Yes, sir. Group say the met forecast for tomorrow is even worse."

A curt nod.

"I think I'll get some fresh air. Thanks."

Villiers watched him stalk out and shook his head.

"Harriet," he muttered to himself, "you know not what you do."

Group Captain Alexander was marching down the corridor as his Squadron Commander emerged from the Adjutant's office.

"Walk?" The older man suggested, tersely. Outside they fell into step. Waiting until he was confident nobody was in earshot he snapped: "You've got a nerve!"

Adam took mild exception to the note of censure.

"We are fighting a war here, sir!"

"I'm fully aware of that! And damn your impertinence!"

Their feet rang dully on the damp tarmac.

"I'm sorry, sir," Adam apologised, for the sake of form. The Old Man was not really angry; he just felt he ought to be.

They strode on in silence for about a hundred yards. "Where's that damned dog of yours?"

"Your driver took him for a walk, sir."

"Did she indeed?" The Group Captain observed. "If Harriet Laing is to be believed, presumably to facilitate some sordid on station liaison!"

Adam let this pass without comment.

"What's this I've heard about young Tilliard requesting a transfer to another squadron?" The older man demanded.

"Ancient history, sir."

"Is it, by God! And you didn't think to mention it to me?

"No, sir."

"You refused to consider his request?"

"He's a first rate pilot."

"I see. So when are you planning to let him start flying ops, again?"

"Next time we're *on*, sir."

"Assuming the boy can find a crew?"

"I don't think that'll be a problem," Adam assured him. The Old Man was disgruntled. Barney Knight had been bending his ear, stirring up Group. The Station Master took these things too personally and the business with the Senior WAAF had brought things to a head. "Peter will be resuming operations with my crew, sir. Well, leaving out the Nav Leader, that is. The chaps have offered to fly a couple of ops with him. That ought to be enough to break the ice. Afterwards, he ought to be able to put together his own crew."

This occasioned a sharp intake of breath on the older man's part: "You ordered your own crew to fly with him?"

Adam looked away.

"No, sir. It was their idea," he explained patiently. "The chaps are free agents, sir." He had signed the orders declaring all six of his crew 'screened– tour expired' before he had been posted to Ansham Wolds. The chaps had volunteered to continue flying ops but he had made it abundantly clear – or rather, he had asked Ben Hardiman to make it abundantly clear to the others – that if at any time they wanted to declare themselves 'tour expired' he would sign the chit 'no questions asked' and they would be free men. "I have first call on them but if I'm not flying an op they are free to fly with anybody they want to. That's how I operated at Waltham Grange, and it is how I will continue to operate here at Ansham Wolds."

"It was their idea?"

"Apparently, sir. The chaps seem to know what they were doing."

Alexander paused for a moment to retrench. Apart from Ben Hardiman, Chantrey's crew were a bolshie lot. A couple of them had already had run ins with B Flight's old lags. The navigation leader was different, a charming fellow who had a happy knack of getting on with everybody.

"So you didn't put them up to it, then?"

"No, sir."

Alexander was unconvinced.

"I don't care for the rivalry that's developing between A and B Flights," he said, out of the blue. "I don't care for it at all!"

"There's nothing wrong with a little inter-flight rivalry, sir."

"It's getting beyond that!"

Adam dug his heels in, determined to tackle the real issue head on. Bert Fulshawe had spoken highly of Alexander, in fact nobody had a bad word to say about him. Because of this and the unhappy circumstances of his posting to 647 Squadron, Adam had been at pains to maintain the closest and most amicable relations with his new Station Master. Nevertheless, *this* particular conversation was overdue and could no longer be avoided.

"With respect, sir. I don't think so. Bert put too much faith in Barney and his people and they let him down. I was sent here to put the Squadron on a proper footing and I will. If Barney doesn't like my methods that's his hard luck. The Squadron will do things my way. B Flight will do things my way. If Barney can't hack it, then he'll have to go!"

The Group Captain picked up his stride as he contemplated his next move. He had already dismissed Knight's complaints out of hand and sent the boy away with rather more than a humble flea in his ear.

"Damn it!" He rumbled. "Damn it, Adam! At least I could have a good old-fashioned shouting match with Bert!"

"Sorry, sir."

They walked on.

"It goes without saying that if you decide to replace Knight you will have my unqualified support."

"Thank you, sir. For the record, I don't want to replace Barney. Any more than I would let a chap like Peter Tilliard go to another squadron." He steeled himself to say what had to be said. "Bert shot himself because he believed, wrongly in my opinion, that he'd killed Peter Tilliard's crew. He was at the end of his tether and he was making a lot of mistakes at the end. Bert was my oldest surviving friend in the world but I won't pretend Bert was some kind of latter day saint, and I won't have Peter Tilliard, or any other old lag on this Squadron treated like a bloody Jeremiad just to vouchsafe Bert's good name." He had stopped in his tracks, swung around to square up to the older man. "Sir!"

"Finished?" The older man asked without a tremor, unblinkingly.

"No, sir. I wish I had more chaps like Peter Tilliard. As for Knight," he shrugged, "Barney hasn't got used to the idea Bert's dead yet. That's why he's behaving like an ass. When we go to the Big City this winter we'll be crying out for chaps like him. And Peter. And all the other fine fellows the Senior WAAF might have in her sights!"

Alexander glared at him. Then, with an abrupt

shake of his head he walked on. The two men fell back into step.

"Sorry," the Station Master said gruffly, "It can't have been much fun for you to have to step into Bert's shoes this way..."

"Better me than a stranger, sir."

"Quite." Alexander lapsed into the quietness of his thoughts. 'When we go to the Big City this winter,' the boy had said, voicing what others left unspoken.

Bomber Command was building up reserves, allowing hard-pressed formations like 647 Squadron to recover, to assimilate replacements, to retrain and rejoin the front line at the highest level of efficiency. The Main Force was on a collision course with its destiny. The final offensive was about to begin and once it began it would be pressed home regardless of the cost. To the bitter end, and if it came to it, to the death.

To the death.

Chapter 16

Thursday 14th October, 1943
The Gatekeeper's Lodge, Ansham Wolds, Lincolnshire

That evening Adam left Rufus with Tom Villiers and drove down to the village. High clouds scudded across a starry sky and the west wind scoured the land as he negotiated the potholed, twisting lane past the Sherwood Arms, below the Church and through the woods that sheltered Eleanor's cottage. Leaves and broken twigs littered the road. The gale rushed noisily through the branches overhead as he got out of the car.

Straightening his battledress tunic he gathered his courage, prepared to knock at the door. He was three-quarters of an hour late. The door opened before he could knock.

"I thought I heard a car," Eleanor beamed. "Do come on in. It looks like it's going to be a stormy night, again?"

"Afraid so," he agreed, stumbling in out of the cold.

"I have a confession to make," the woman admitted.

"Really?"

"I wasn't sure if you'd come tonight."

He held up his hands.

"Well, here I am!"

"And I'm glad you're here!"

On tip toes Eleanor planted a light, pecking kiss on his cheek. Taking his hand in hers she drew him out of the narrow hallway, into the parlour where the fire crackled and sizzled in the big, wide hearth. Instantly, the man forgot the cares and woes of the Squadron. The woman smiled at him and he was happily bewitched. Within the four walls of the old cottage he was perfectly insulated from the realities of the outside world.

"I'm sorry I'm so late," he apologized.

Eleanor neither expected, nor wanted to hear words

of apology. Yes, she had worried when he had not appeared at the appointed hour. And yes, she would have much preferred him not to have been late. However, she had already decided that such things would not intrude into their time together. Before the war she would have flown at him for treating her thus, but that was then and this was now. Nothing was normal, now. She had become involved with him - freely and knowingly - and in letting it happen, she had accepted that there was little she could ask of him in return. Adam Chantrey would never be at her beck and call. Neither in war, nor peace. And she would have been a fool to herself to have expected anything else.

"No," she said, putting a finger to his lips. "No. It doesn't matter. I'm just glad you could get away."

Adam gazed at her, not knowing what to say.

She laughed softly, fondly.

"It won't ever matter if you're late. Or if you have to cry off. Yes, I'll be a little upset, and lonely perhaps. But it won't ever *matter*."

He remained tongue-tied, bewildered.

"You see, I know that you're not a free man." Before he could disagree she went on. "You're already married: to the Squadron."

"I get time off for good behaviour."

"I'm just saying I'm under no illusions. That's all." They looked at each other. "Besides," she added, "I've only this minute got Johnny and Emmy off to bed. So you couldn't have timed your arrival any better if you wanted to."

"I'm still sorry I'm late."

"Apology accepted, Wing-Commander."

They dissolved into giggles, in a moment he had wrapped her in his arms and they were kissing. She fought him off, half-heartedly, laughing with pleasure.

"Wing-Commander?" He chuckled.

"Adam." She raised her mouth to his, her lips lightly

brushing his. "Now, if you want to eat tonight you're going to have to let go of me."

Reluctantly, he released her.

"I've laid the table for two in the kitchen. Come with me, we can talk while I get on with things." Eleanor sat him at the sturdy oak table and busied herself with the pans on the low wood-burning range. The smell of stew simmering on the hot plate filled the room.

"I hope you're hungry?"

The aroma of the stew made Adam go weak at the knees.

"I should say!"

"Good. When Harry, my husband, was sent overseas he insisted I brought the children back to Ansham. You see, food's not such a problem here in the country, there's always rabbit and game birds. Everybody has their own vegetable patch, the local farmers are always ready to sell or barter eggs, meat, most things really. Now and then we have to rely on our ration books but mostly, we eat very well. I'm luckier than most of course. Even though Harry was the last of the Grafton's and the Grafton Estate no longer exists, a lot of the older folk around here still remember the days when Harry's father was Squire. Some of them, as odd as it may seem, rather fondly."

Adam noted the irony in the remark, let it pass. Ansham Wolds beyond the boundaries of the aerodrome remained a mystery to him. He knew virtually nothing of its history and less still about the Grafton family or its fortunes.

"Your husband's family owned the big house up the road, then?"

"Yes," she said, looking up from her pans. "The Wall Street crash bankrupted Harry's father long before I came on the scene. The family held on for a few years but eventually the bank stepped in and that was the end of the Graftons of Ansham Wolds. The big house was abandoned in 1934. I believe part of the estate survived as a working entity until just before the war. It has all gone to rack and ruin. Harry said the shame of it killed his father."

Eleanor took plates from the cupboard and put them in the oven to warm. The heat from the range raised a flush in her cheeks, disturbed her raven black hair, and blew long strands out of place.

"Your people come from Oxford, of course," Adam prompted, watching her from afar, put at his ease by the soothing balm of her voice. "Was that where you met Harry, your husband?"

"Yes. Harry was a frustrated actor and a girlfriend of mine was a member of his amateur dramatic society," she explained. "She kept telling me about this lovely, eccentric man who directed all their productions and eventually we were introduced. He was four years older than me. He took a shine to me straight away. I was a bit offish to start with, but when I realised what a nice man he was, we became friends. It wasn't love at first sight or anything, but things sort of developed between us. As they do. I'd never met anybody quite like him. He had so many ideas. So many dreams. He was dreadfully idealistic, naive really, I suppose. Anyway, a couple of years later we were married. That was in thirty-six. But for the war we'd have probably lived happily ever afterwards. But there we go. It wasn't to be and you have to get on with things, whatever happens. Don't you think?" It was exactly what Adam thought and Eleanor took his silence as an eloquent token of agreement. "I never knew Harry's parents, and there weren't any brothers or sisters. Do you have any family?"

The directness of the question startled the man out of his shell.

"My father," he blurted, "Sir Evelyn, owns land in Cornwall. The family still has various mining and quarrying interests in the West Country. I'm afraid he and I don't see eye to eye over very much these days, so we do the decent thing and keep well out of each other's way. Mother died before the war. Paul, my brother was killed during the Battle of Britain. He was a Spitfire pilot. He was shot down over Kent. I've got three older sisters, all married. They all married well, you know, to chaps in protected occupations."

"Lots of nieces and nephews?"

"Oh, hordes of the little beggars!"

Eleanor glanced over her shoulder.

"Is that where your people are from? Cornwall?"

"Yes. Father lives in the family pile outside Bodmin."

"It's beautiful down there."

"Yes."

Eleanor paused, smiled. "So, you're the youngest?"

He nodded.

"I thought you probably were," she declared, wryly triumphant.

"How so?"

"I just knew! I sometimes have these feelings about people. And I just knew."

"Woman's intuition?"

At this she laughed.

"Harry used say it was because my mother was a witch!"

Adam blinked, searched desperately for a safe reply. He considered a number of alternatives and then, without knowing why, asked something completely different.

"And was she?"

Again, the woman laughed.

"A witch? Possibly. Mother was a rather unconventional woman. Before she met my father she was on the stage. Very Bloomsbury Set. It's not really a thing the family talks about but I gather from my aunts that mother's lifestyle in the old days used to be, shall we say, a tad Bohemian." And proudly. "Quite scandalous, by all accounts."

Eleanor knelt to get the plates out of the oven. She began to serve from the pans on the range. Presently, she placed a brimming plate before the man. Potatoes and mashed turnip sat in a steaming sea of game stew.

"I should imagine being married to my father for thirty years would be enough to turn any woman into a witch," she decided, dryly. "Don't wait for me, tuck in."

Later, sipping cocoa in front of the fire, Eleanor risked a question she suspected she ought not to ask but two small glasses of the Rector's pea pod wine had made her reckless.

"The other day, you said my father tried to have you cashiered?"

Adam had sunk into the armchair and was staring into the flames in the hearth. It was dark in the parlour, the only light coming from a low candle and the fire. He looked across to her. The woman was sitting on the rug, her skirts spread around her.

"We had a small difference of opinion," he murmured.

Eleanor saw the shutters slam shut, recognised instantly that he had said everything he intended to say on the matter. For the moment, at least.

"I'm sorry. I shouldn't have asked."

"It's all right." Adam's voice was distracted, his thoughts elsewhere.

The day he took command at Waltham Grange he discovered 388 Squadron was trialling an experimental 'night fighter proximity warning device', designed by the Prof's pet boffins. The apparatus allegedly detected an approaching night fighter's radar transmissions. The Squadron was in the middle of a bad run, the start of which had corresponded with the commencement of the trials of the so-called 'warning device'. Adam ought to have halted the trial then and there. Instead, he had allowed it to continue another month. The faces of the missing haunted him yet. Finally, he had sent the Group Commander a short, damning report on the efficacy of the device as a 'fighter homing beacon', and ordered the apparatus to be removed from his Lancasters.

The Deputy AOC had summoned him to Group Headquarters to haul him over the coals – backwards and forwards several times - for 'wrecking' the trial. Harangued him with rare style and poise until he ran out of breath. Adam had almost been impressed. Almost.

'Nevertheless, sir,' he had declared, 'I won't have this device on my aircraft. It has killed quite enough of my people, already!'

The Deputy AOC had gone red in the face and tersely reminded him that the prerogative to abort the operational trials of new equipment did not lie with within the competence of 'lowly Squadron Commanders'.

'Then, with respect, sir. You must replace me. While I command 388 Squadron this device will not be installed on my aircraft!'

Within forty-eight hours Adam had received a second summons to Bawtry Hall. This time to be ticked off by the AOC, in person.

'You're a damned fool, Chantrey!'

'Yes, sir.'

'There are channels.'

'Going through proper channels takes time, sir. In the meantime my crews were being killed, needlessly. Sir!'

The AOC had pursed his thin, pale lips, viewed him coldly.

'The Air Ministry wants you court-martialed. The Chief won't have it, of course. For what it's worth, neither will I. However, the next time you decide to take matters into your own hands God help you! Do I make myself clear?'

'Yes, sir...'

That was only three months ago; since then so much bloodied water had passed under the bridge it seemed already like it had happened in another century.

"Hello, remember me?" Eleanor chided, gently.

"Sorry, I was miles away."

"In future I shall try not to ask you any of those 'how was your day at the office, darling?' type of questions."

"That would probably be the wisest thing," he agreed wryly.

Chapter 17

Friday 15th October, 1943
RAF Ansham Wolds, Lincolnshire

After midnight Adam stopped off at his office. Ben Hardiman was propped up on two chairs, moderately drunk and snoring loudly, fast asleep. The big man blinked awake when he slammed the door.

"God, what time is it?"

"Late."

Ben swung his legs to the floor. "How was your evening?" He inquired, groggily.

Adam reflected for a moment. Although they had never spoken of it, he had always assumed that Ben was in the know about his fling with Helen Fulshawe. Anybody serving with him in the old days would have known that there was a woman in the background and that whoever she was, he was in her thrall. The identity of his 'mystery woman' had been the subject of a sweepstake run by his old lags on 380 Squadron at Kelmington the previous autumn. The names of likely candidates had been pulled out of the hat. It was well meant, but Helen's name had been one of those in the hat and the news had got back to her. It was probably the final nail in the coffin. That and the fact Kelmington had killed the man Helen had fallen in love with, left her with his shadow, an emptied husk of the man who had taken off for Wilhelmshaven all those years ago, and turned her lover into a brooding, solitary stranger.

"My evening? Fine," Adam declared, sitting on the edge of his desk. "Fine. I've been meaning to talk to you about Peter Tilliard. You're not miffed about the chaps planning to fly a couple of ops with Peter?"

The big man rubbed his eyes.

"No, course not. I think it's a bloody good thing. Peter's a good sort. People are saying you put the chaps up to it?"

Adam held up his hands in mock surrender.

"Nothing to do with me, old man. Scout's honour. The first I heard about it was when Peter said the chaps had volunteered to fly with him."

Ben regarded him bleary-eyed.

"Okay," he muttered, heaving himself upright. If the Skipper had not put the chaps up to it then the explanation must lie somewhere among the whispers he had heard about a certain fracas in Scunthorpe outside *The Liberty*. Peter Tilliard had allegedly intervened to keep the chaps out of the clutches of the local constabulary. By all accounts Peter had played the 'me an officer and a gentlemen and you humble bobbies – be off with you and stop pestering my chaps' card and saved the day. Or rather, the night. The chaps would have appreciated a thing like that and quite naturally felt honour bound to return the favour.

"One thing, though," the big man remarked.

"Oh, what's that?"

"If you don't wipe that bloody smile off your face people around here are going to start thinking you're human after all!" Ben grinned at him, sniffed, swayed on his feet. "She's a real lady. It's good to see you in such good form, Skipper. Bloody good!"

"Get out of here!" Adam laughed.

In the quiet of the office he settled at his desk and by the light of the single, glaring overhead lamp began to pick through his in tray. He smoked a cigarette, it was impossible to concentrate on the paperwork. Eleanor's face appeared on every page, her brown eyes shining, twinkling. The scent of her filled his senses and the echo of her voice lingered in his ears. It was as if she was with him still, wherever he went.

Without meaning to he had talked to her about last year at Kelmington, confided things about those terrible days he had never told anybody. Sleepy Kelmington, hidden in the remnants of Robin Hood's Sherwood Forest within sight, almost in the shadow of Lincoln's great hill top cathedral on the flood plain of the River Trent.

'They'd been flying Halifaxes,' he'd recounted, 'and were in the middle of converting to Lancs. So I took my Boscombe Test Flight, Dave and the others, lock, stock and barrel up to Kelmington in July last year. There were already a number of chaps I knew on the Squadron. I poached a few more chums, that sort of thing was tolerated in those days. Nowadays, poaching is frowned upon, somewhat. Strictly *verboten*, actually. Anyway, by the end of August we'd converted to Lancs. It was a good time. The best of times, as they say. Trouble was when we got down to ops we seemed to lose chaps every week. On ops, in accidents. I'd had a spell in command of a night fighter squadron, Beaufighters, that spring, but Kelmington was my first time in command of a bomber squadron. I wrote an awful lot of letters. For a while I'm afraid I rather lost my sense of humour...'

Eleanor had listened, let him talk until he had got it off his chest. Later, she changed the subject completely and asked him half in jest, whether he thought his father would approve of her.

'Why wouldn't he?'

'Well,' she reminded him. 'I am several years older than you. Families often get very touchy about older women taking advantage of their sons, especially when they're eligible. How old are you, by the way?'

'Twenty-five. Twenty-six in February...'

'Oh, I'm only six years older, then. Well, nearly seven, actually...'

'I wouldn't say I'm very eligible,' he protested. 'In fact I'd say my prospects are a tad uncertain, wouldn't you?'

'No. I'd say you're very, very eligible.'

He and his father were estranged and he had not visited the family home in Bodmin since before the war.

For all he knew his father had cut him adrift. As for his sisters, his correspondence with them was sporadic although he remained close to Henrietta, who was only eighteen months his senior. Whenever he went down to Cornwall he stayed with Henrietta and her brood, in the big old house in Tavistock.

Eleanor's mother's people came from Vienna.

Her family had lost touch with the Austrian relatives a year or so before the war.

'They were well off. They could have left at any time after Hitler came to power but if they had they would have lost everything. Besides, Vienna was their home. I know Father tried to persuade them to come to this country.'

'When I was young,' Adam had volunteered, 'Paul and I and the girls were packed off to Germany every summer. To Bavaria, Munich, when I was about nine or ten. Berlin, when I was older. Right up to the outbreak of war I was still writing to my German friends and pen pals. Practising my German. When I was fifteen I fell in love with a girl call Inge. Her brother was a Brown Shirt. An odious, spotty fellow. He liked shouting.' He felt almost guilty that he retained, even now, such fond memories of those childhood days with the families of his father's German business partners. 'Odd, isn't it? The last time I visited Berlin I dropped a bloody great big cookie and several hundred incendiaries along the Unter den Linden from a very great height!'

Eleanor had got up from the rug in front of the fire and sat on the arm of his chair, looking down on him.

'And are you still in love with Inge?'

'No, I got over her a long time ago.'

'But sometimes you still think about her?'

'Only when I visit Berlin. She broke my heart!'

Eleanor's hazel brown eyes had fixed on him.

'I can see I shall have to be careful not to make the same mistake.' She had leaned on him, and he had circled her waist, drawn her onto his lap and cradled her in his arms. They had stayed like that, quietly close, unconscious of the passage of time until the clock on the mantelpiece chimed the midnight hour and broke the spell. They had kissed goodnight in the doorway.

'When shall I see you next?' Eleanor had breathed.

'When may I see you next?' He had whispered in her ear.

'Whenever you want, of course.'

'Soon, I hope.'

'Good. Take care...'

Adam stubbed out his cigarette.

It was cold in his office.

Chapter 18

Sunday 17th October, 1943
St. Paul's Church, Ansham Wolds, Lincolnshire

Group Captain Alexander and his Squadron Commander hurried up the path to the church, shook the Reverend Naismith-Parry's hand, exchanged brief pleasantries and went inside. Their arrival turned heads, gave rise to a murmur of voices. The Group Captain took his place in his normal pew, near the back. Adam however, joined Eleanor and her children at the front of the congregation. The murmurings swelled, echoed to the rafters.

"Sorry I'm so late," he whispered, accepting the hymn book she pressed into his hands. "Hello, you two," he said, softly, to Johnny and Emmy, meeting their wide curious eyes as he took his seat. Turning to Eleanor he confessed his unease at being the object of so much attention. "I didn't realise the whole village would be here."

"Never mind," Eleanor said, patting his hand, serenely.

Around mid-day she had heard a car draw up outside the cottage. Opening the door she was a little disappointed to find a young WAAF in the porch.

"Wing-Commander Chantrey said I was to hand this letter to Mrs Eleanor Grafton, ma'am," the girl had explained.

"That's me."

"Thank goodness, I thought I was lost."

Eleanor had torn open the envelope, read the neat, flowing script of the note within.

> *Dear Eleanor,*
> *May I accompany you to Evensong this evening? ACW Mills will bring back your reply if*

this is not convenient, or if you feel
together 'in public', as it were, would
way inappropriate at this time.

    Adam

Now Eleanor sat in the ancestral pew
family with her *beau*. They would be ~~the talk of the~~
village tomorrow. How tongues would wag! Across the
aisle Adelaide Naismith-Parry beamed maternally,
proudly in her direction. Eleanor felt a pang of guilt, she
ought to have warned Adam, stopped him proclaiming to
the whole world that they were sweethearts. At least for
a little while longer.

The distant sound of Merlin engines filtered into the
church. Many engines straining for height over the
village, growing louder, louder until the roar began to set
panes of glass rattling and the air itself trembling.

"Nothing to worry about," Adam whispered, leaning
close to the woman. "Barney's taking some of his chaps
off to Wales for a spot of fighter affiliation."

"Oh."

Eleanor listened to the Lancasters climbing in the
dusk over Lincolnshire. 'Fighter affiliation' was RAF talk
for playing hide and seek with Fighter Command. Her
brother had chattered endlessly about these things in
his letters. Latterly, she wished she had paid rather
more than lip service to his tales of derring-do. With
Dave everything was a 'wizard prang', or a 'dodgy show'
or a 'real party'. In retrospect she had foolishly taken his
optimistic, Devil may care pretence rather too much at
face value.

Eleanor's thoughts wandered. She had married
Harry Grafton in a Registry Office. Had she known then
about Ansham Wolds and this beautiful old church on
the hill she would never have consented to a drab,
hurried wedding in a grey Registry Office in Oxford. Next
time. If there was a next time, it would be in church.

church...

Eleanor paused, instantly taking herself to task for having allowed herself to think the unthinkable. She blushed deeply, lowered her eyes and thanked her lucky stars that the entrance of the Rector meant her blush went unnoticed. The congregation rose as the Rector and his sidesmen, led by the stooped figure of Edward Rowbotham - Ansham Wolds's ARP Commissar - in his ill-fitting suit, followed by the old men and boys of the choir, progressed slowly down the aisle to take their places.

The Chief ARP Warden took his seat at the rear of the choir stalls. No matter how hard he tried not to look, he could not stop himself stealing involuntary glances at the Grafton pew and the uniformed person of its newest occupant.

Eleanor caught him stealing a glance in her direction.

She smiled, patted Adam's hand happily and for the umpteenth time that day she told herself to take things step by step; and to beware of taking *anything* for granted.

Chapter 19

Sunday 17th October, 1943
RAF Ansham Wolds, Lincolnshire

Group Captain Alexander's eyes were still adjusting to the darkness when the stricken Lancaster made its first approach. High overhead a dazzling red flare exploded.

Following Evensong the Group Captain had gone back to the Rectory, taken tea with the Reverend Naismith-Parry and his wife, and not returned to the station until after nine. The Rector's conversation, although occasionally contentious was always stimulating and an hour or so in the elderly couple's company was a marvellously pleasant distraction from the starkness of life on the aerodrome. On his return he had headed straight for his room, got on with some paperwork until the Adjutant put his head around the door to warn him there was a flap on.

A problem with one of B Flight's aircraft.

Winded from climbing the watchtower steps Alexander listened to the latest report. One half of B Flight had been despatched on a cross-country trip across the Midlands to north Wales. This part of the night's training programme had been closely co-ordinated with Fighter Command, the route, height and speed of the bombers carefully plotted to accommodate affiliation evolutions with radar-equipped Mosquito night fighters. This exercise seemed to have gone exactly to plan. The returning crews had reported a number of visual contacts with twin-engine aircraft, and all six Lancasters had now landed safely. The rest of the Flight, five aircraft, had been tasked to fly a navigation exercise to the north of Scotland and back. The route had been cleared, in writing, by the Group Army Liaison Officer, twenty-four hours in advance of the exercise.

"P-Popsie, sir," Barney Knight reported, grimly.

"There'll be Hell to pay for this! South of York." He was not so much speaking as *spitting*. "A whole bloody battery opened up. Hit a couple of the other kites but P-Popsie got the worst of it. Lost her port inner. Lots of fuel, too. Bugger all hydraulic pressure. Bloody Army!"

"I take it P-Popsie and the other aircraft were on track? IFF on?"

Identification Friend or Foe was a device which should have warned any gunner laying radar-directed fire on the bombers that he was shooting at friendly aircraft.

"Right on the nail, sir!" Knight retorted, spitting mad. "Six thousand feet flying *Gee* fixes, with IFF *and* their bloody nav lights on!"

Like the Flight Commander, Alexander also wanted blood. Somebody's, anybody's would do. Unlike Knight, he was prepared to wait for his pound of flesh. Morning would be soon enough. The immediate priority was to get P-Popsie down in one piece.

"Has Wing-Commander Chantrey returned to the station?"

"Yes, sir." This from the Adjutant.

"Do we know where he is?"

"His batman says he and the Nav Leader went for a walk, sir."

"Glasses, please." Somebody handed the Group Captain a pair of binoculars. It was a clear, starry night and the bomber was visible in the distance by the light of the waning Moon. Its first approach was thoroughly botched and nearly ended in disaster.

"Too fast!"

"Too steep!"

The pilot must have realized the approach was all wrong. The power came on and P-Popsie clawed away into the night, hauling around for a second attempt. In front of the hangars the fire wagons and ambulances revved their engines.

When the first red flare had ignited high in the night sky Adam and Ben Hardiman were walking Rufus out by the far dispersals.

Earlier that evening Adam had lingered awhile outside the Church, talking with Eleanor about nothing in particular.

'Ah, Mr Rowbotham!' She had announced, breaking off. 'Wing-Commander, may I introduce you to the village's Chief ARP Warden.'

Adam had shaken the older man's hand, and made an effort to be civil.

'How do you do, Mr Rowbotham. You fellows do sterling work.'

The ARP Warden seemed ill at ease.

'Thank you, sir,' he muttered, before scurrying away.

Eleanor smiled.

'What is it?' Adam had asked, grinning.

'Nothing. It's nothing. Really.'

Adam had bidden her goodnight shortly afterwards.

He disliked being away from the station when so many of his heavies were in the air and he hoped Eleanor understood.

"I wonder who it is?" Ben thought, out aloud.

The two old lags had viewed the crippled Lancaster's first attempt to land without emotion, divorced from the grim actuality of the drama. The last aircraft from Barney's section had landed forty minutes ago. Both men knew that they were witnessing sprogs fighting for their lives. Ben got out a crumpled pack of cigarettes, Woodbines. Matches flared in the darkness.

"Do you think we ought to head on back to the watchtower?"

Adam shook his head. "No. We'd only get in the way."

"Look," Ben began, cut himself off, briefly thinking better of it. "There's something I've been meaning to tell you."

"Oh, what's that?" Ben's awkwardness should have warned Adam something was awry but he was focussing on the stricken aircraft. The Lancaster was making a second landing approach.

"About what the chaps are saying about Bert Fulshawe."

Half a mile away P-Popsie swept over the perimeter fence.

"Sorry, what are they saying about Bert?" Adam inquired, distractedly, eying the Lancaster in the middle distance. "That's it," he mouthed. "That's it. Lots and lots of revs. Don't be afraid to keep the revs up. Keep off the elevator, that's it..."

P-Popsie's wheels hit the runway. There was an agonized squeal of tortured rubber, the muted detonation of a tyre bursting. The Lancaster, twenty tons of her, bounced high into the air. There she hung for a moment, a long, long moment before she fell to earth. Travelling forward at over a hundred knots the bomber pancaked into the runway. The undercarriage sheared, disintegrated, the great, three-bladed propellers spinning at thousands of revs a minute struck the tarmac, deformed, and flew to pieces. P-Popsie slewed around on her crushed belly, a shower of crimson sparks flying in her wake as she careered onto the muddy infield, gouging a ragged furrow. It was over in seconds.

The wreck came to a standstill in the mire, steaming evilly. Mercifully, there was no fire. The banshee wailing of sirens called out across the high wold as fire wagons, ambulances and recovery trucks raced each other to be the first to arrive at the crash.

"I've seen better landings," Ben observed in a tone which, to an outsider, would have seemed unspeakably callous.

"I should bloody well hope so, old man!" Adam turned to meet his friend's eye. "You said you've been meaning to tell me something?"

Ben rubbed his chin, sucked his teeth.

"The chaps in the Mess are saying Helen Fulshawe was having an affair."

"Go on?" Adam invited, groping for his silver cigarette case. The one Helen had given him a week after he and Ben had shot down the first of their four night fighter kills on that long ago night in 1941.

"With an ops type."

Belatedly remembering he already had a cigarette in his hand Adam jammed Helen's cigarette case back in his pocket, viewed his friend with what he hoped might be construed as poker-faced detachment.

"The thing is," Ben said, gazing across the airfield to where the fire wagons and ambulances were gathering around the crashed Lancaster. "They're saying there was a letter in his desk," the big man continued, grimly. "Pretty much a blow by blow account, I gather. Poison pen job. Anonymous, of course, dated three days before his death. It seems some chump on the Committee of Adjustment section got a bit worse for wear in the Mess the other night, and let the cat out the bag."

Inwardly, Adam's thoughts were in turmoil. Outwardly, the mask never slipped an inch. Bert had known about him and Helen. Bert had been on the edge for weeks. The discovery would have been the final straw. It was a nightmare...

"No names, no pack drill?"

"No. I've made one or two unofficial enquiries but Bert's personal effects have already been bagged up and lodged with Group. Sorry."

"Thanks for trying, anyway."

Ben sniffed the cool night air. Across the field the flare path lights began to wink out. Adam shivered.

"Don't you go blaming yourself," the big man said, quietly. "Bert was riding for a fall. Had been for a while. If it hadn't been the letter it would have been something else. You know what it's like when a chap gets twitchy.

Slippery slope and all that."

"I need a drink," Adam decided, hardening his heart.

Chapter 20

Monday 18th October, 1943
No. 1 Group Headquarters, Bawtry Hall, South Yorkshire

The Deputy Group Commander did not look up when Group Captain Alexander and Wing-Commander Chantrey were ushered into his office. Both men stood at attention, saluted crisply. Air Commodore Crowe-Martin put down his pen, viewed them bleakly.

"The Army is hopping mad!" He scowled, looking first to the Station Master, then to the younger man. "There are channels. Appropriate channels!"

Adam sighed. So that was what all this was about.

Barney Knight had gone looking for somebody to blame in the small hours of the morning. Little of what he had had to say about the Army in general, and the brown types manning a certain anti-aircraft battery on the outskirts of York in particular was repeatable in mixed company.

"Who does Knight think he is?" Demanded the Deputy AOC, irascibly. "Is the man completely brainless?"

Adam coughed.

"Squadron Leader Knight," he replied, evenly, "is an exceptionally able and experienced officer, sir."

Air Commodore Crowe-Martin glowered at the younger man. The AOC gave the boy too much licence, he was a loose cannon. If something was not done he would become a liability. He had said as much to the Group Commander but much to his chagrin, his views had been politely, firmly, unambiguously rebuffed. The AOC, normally the least sentimental of men, had a blind spot a mile wide when it came to Adam Chantrey.

Group Captain Alexander listened to the exchange in silence, horrified.

When neither of his elders said a word, Adam went

on.

"Squadron Leader Knight is an exceptionally able and experienced officer," he repeated, calmly. "Who enjoys my full and unqualified confidence. Sir!"

"Does he by god!" Air Commodore Crowe-Martin snapped. "Damn it, Chantrey! We can't have our chaps accusing the Army of murder! We can't have junior officers ringing up generals in the middle of the night and telling them what he thinks of them! It's not done!"

"No, sir."

"Damn it. We're supposed to be on the same side!"

"Yes, sir." Adam acknowledged, although he sometimes privately he harboured doubts.

Barney Knight had dug himself a deep pit last night. His second-in-command had got through to the divisional commander of the battery responsible for firing on his sprogs. Not content with getting a major general out of bed in the middle of the night he had given him a piece of his mind. Adam had only caught the tail end of the conversation.

'...Oh, that takes the biscuit! You call it what you want, chum! I call it cold blooded murder! That's what I call it! There wasn't a German aircraft within two hundred miles! Reasonable? You're asking me to be reasonable! Look, chum. Every time my chaps come back from Germany - you know, where the enemy is - some trigger happy brown type takes a pot shot at one of them! Take it from me, old son, the novelty wears off after a while! Unlike you chaps, we're used to being shot at because we've been fighting the Jerries for years! Anytime you chaps want to join in that's fine by me! Until then I'd be obliged if you'd stop shooting at my bloody Lancs...'

"The AOC is hopping mad!" Crowe-Martin rasped. "Inter-service rivalry is a touchy thing. Damned touchy. Channels exist to avoid this sort of situation!"

Adam looked directly ahead. Outside the morning

mist was lifting and bright autumnal sunshine broke over the faded greenery of the landscape beyond the sprawl of huts below Bawtry Hall. He could not help but reflect on the irony of his situation.

Last night the Army had opened fire on five of his aircraft: two of his sprogs were dead, two more in hospital, one of his Lancasters had been written off, and another damaged so seriously it was unlikely to be available for ops for weeks rather than days. Yet while there was not so much as a scintilla of a suggestion that he, or that any man under his command was in any way culpable, it was not beyond the realms of possibility that the Deputy AOC had been ordered to find a scapegoat to placate the Army's offended sensibilities.

Group Captain Alexander was thinking the same thought and he was outraged. Anger brought forth the lion heart in him. He cleared his throat, loudly. Pointedly.

"Excuse me, sir."

"Yes, what is it, Alex?" Snapped the Deputy AOC, tetchily.

"I had assumed you'd asked Wing-Commander Chantrey and myself to Group Headquarters to discuss operational matters, sir," he said, gruffly. "May I suggest that if inter-service co-operation is to be discussed that the Group Army Liaison Officer be included in the discussion. I for one would like to ask him why five of *my* aircraft, flying a route cleared through *his* office, were fired on last night? And while we're about it, what disciplinary measures are to be taken against the *Army* officer, or officers, responsible for last night's cock up?"

The Deputy Group Commander stared daggers at Alexander.

Alcxander went on: "While I regret that in the heat of the moment, a junior officer under my command made certain ill-advised remarks to a senior officer of *another* service, it seems obvious to me that last night's cock up was caused by failings at Group. Furthermore, my report on last night's events will reflect this view. As for Knight's conduct, I think it is a matter best dealt with locally. Kept within the family. I take full responsibility for his actions. Full responsibility, sir."

"Do you, indeed!"

"Yes, sir."

The Deputy AOC's eyes narrowed. He had had enough of the charade. Alexander's obduracy and Chantrey's thinly-disguised insubordination rankled but deep down, he was whole-heartedly behind the AOC's point blank refusal to censure either man. The AOC was fed up with the Army shooting down his heavies. Fed up to the back teeth.

"Damn it!" Air Commodore Crowe-Martin sighed, wearily. "For the record, the AOC has communicated to me his desire that Squadron Leader Knight should be reminded, urgently, and that in future he is to restrict himself to the appropriate channels. There must be no further incidents of this kind. I repeat. No further incidents, gentlemen. As for pacifying the Army, the AOC feels that whatever the rights or wrongs, we must 'go through the motions'. If only to retain the moral high ground, as it were. Somebody from Ansham Wolds will have to go up to York and smooth ruffled feathers. That I leave in your capable hands, Alex."

In the corridor Adam glanced at Alexander.

"Don't say a word," growled the Group Captain, stiffly. "Not a single word!"

Chapter 21

Monday 18th October, 1943
Lancaster B-Beer, 15 miles NW of Texel

B-Beer climbed high into the night. The sky was black, cold and empty all the way to the stars. Her Merlins sang their brutal song. The intercom hissed.

"Navigator to pilot."

"Pilot to navigator," Peter Tilliard drawled in acknowledgement. After spending the best part of a month on the sidelines he was mightily relieved to be back on ops. Albeit back on ops and still saddled with the Conversion Flight. Not that he was complaining. True to his word the Wingco had let him back on ops the moment the Flight Surgeon gave him the green light. "What can I do for you, Jack?"

Flight-Lieutenant Jack Gordon chuckled to himself, flicked his intercom switch. "Any idea where we're supposed to be going tonight, Skipper?"

Tilliard grinned. Jack had approached him in the Mess within hours of it becoming known that five members of the Wingco's crew had volunteered to fly ops with him. Gordon was an Australian who had been living in Britain at the outbreak of war. Twenty-seven years old and Sydney-born, he had thus far successfully rebutted all attempts by his native land to reclaim him. Much as he loved the land of his birth he had lived half his life in the British Isles and if he had wanted to join the Royal Australian Air Force he would have done so of his own accord by now. Having arrived at Ansham Wolds direct from instructing at OTU he had survived six ops with scratch crews.

"Some place called Hanover, I think, Jack. Over."

"Right you are, Skipper. As long as it's on the map we should be okay then!"

"Rear-gunner to nav," chipped in Taffy Davies. "Can

I have that in writing?"

"You got any spare toilet paper, mate?"

Tilliard let the banter continue. His first conversation with Jack Gordon stuck in his mind.

'Lindholme instructor, eh? You must be a decent sort of pilot, mate,' Jack had observed. 'That's good enough for me. They say you've got bloody good taste in Sheilas, too. Pity you're a pommy bastard, but two out of three ain't bad. So, how about it? Do I get the job?'

Tilliard, although a little unnerved by the fact that news of his stuttering romance with Suzy seemed to be all over the station, had nevertheless retained the presence of mind to accept the Australian's offer to join his crew with undignified alacrity.

For his part Jack Gordon was counting his blessings. Opportunities to fly with a crew of old lags - and these chaps were mostly old lags of the hardest of hard-bitten types - were few and far between these days and under no circumstances to be scorned. He concentrated on the indistinct white blur of the Dutch coast sliding across the small, flickering screen of his *H2S* set.

"Nav to pilot," Jack announced, abruptly curtailing the tomfoolery. "It's about now we're supposed to start *Windowing*."

"Pilot to bomb-aimer," Tilliard called. "Did you hear that Round Again?"

Normally, W/T Operators on Lancasters drew the short straw and the *'Windowing'* duty. However, Ted Hallowes had quietly advised his new pilot that the Wingco preferred Bert Pound to 'play the frequencies' looking for and jamming German night fighter transmissions. Bert, it seemed, was something of a dab hand at the game and the CO took the view that he was wasted *Windowing*. 'Besides,' Hallowes had remarked, dryly, *'Windowing* keeps Round Again busy on the route out. It stops him getting over-excited, if you catch my drift.'

"Commence *Windowing*, roger, Skipper!"

Tilliard suspected that this was one of those nights when only luck stood between the Main Force and catastrophe. *Window* worked best on the dirtiest of nights, hardly at all on nights like this. The stars in the sky twinkled brightly and up ahead the boiling contrails of scores of heavies signposted the way to Germany. This was perfect night fighter weather.

"Turning point in four minutes, Skipper!" Jack warned.

Tilliard could see at least half-a-dozen other heavies. Below, ahead, and above B-Beer perfectly silhouetted against the stars and the contrails, in plain view. There were supposed to be clouds, instead the sky was cold, clear and horrifyingly dangerous.

"Pilot to navigator," he acknowledged. "Roger. I can see the openers turning."

There was a moment's delay. Then Jack Gordon confirmed that he was precisely attuned to his new pilot's wavelength.

"Not good, Skipper."

The Lancaster Force, operating at maximum effort, was wheeling past Emden, flooding across the German border, arrowing north of the Ruhr and rolling, rumbling, thundering directly towards Hanover. In the distance flames in the sky marked the fall of heavies and flak lit up the southern horizon. Somebody was lost, that was Osnabruck down in the south. The straggler was coned in the searchlights and methodically hacked to pieces by the guns of a whole city.

Jack made a brief appearance by the pilot's shoulder to stretch his legs. He eyed the sky.

"Nice night for it!" He shouted above the roar of the Merlins, swiftly re-clipping his oxygen mask over his face.

"Heavy going down at two o'clock!" Reported Bob

Marshall, from the mid-upper turret. "Range four miles."

Tilliard tried even harder to shut out distractions. He weaved the bomber from side to side, allowing the yaw to roll the heavy up to ten degrees to port and starboard, giving his gunners every opportunity to search the sky below for danger.

Periodically, S-Sugar rocked in the slipstream of another Lancaster.

"Thirty minutes to the target, Skipper!"

Chapter 22

Tuesday 19th October, 1943
RAF Ansham Wolds, Lincolnshire

Adam breathed a heartfelt sigh of relief as Peter Tilliard and his crew trudged wearily into the hall. Several other crews were still waiting to be de-briefed, drinking cocoa, smoking, talking lowly amongst themselves. A WAAF, the Station Master's driver, approached the newcomers bearing a tray of steaming mugs. Adam was so relieved to see Tilliard and the others that he did not think the girl's presence at all odd.

"Hello, gentlemen," she smiled.

Jack Gordon, Tilliard's Australian navigator, slapped his pilot on the back.

"That's what it's all about, Skipper," he chuckled. "Service with a smile!"

Tilliard threw him a frown.

"Are you always this bloody cheerful, Jack?"

"Afraid so!"

"Hello, Peter," Adam called, joining the crew huddle. "Everything go okay?"

"Well, we got back, sir!"

"So I see. I gather the Met boys got it wrong, again?"

"Yes, sir. Clear as a bell all the way to the target then ten-tenths cloud over the aiming point. Markers were going down all over the shop. Jack wasn't able to identify any ground features from *H2S* indications so we couldn't even do a time and distance bombing run. I should imagine the Pathfinders had the same problem. We ended up heading for the middle of the searchlight area and unloading more or less dead centre. Goodness knows what we actually bombed."

"These things happen," Adam commiserated. "Pressing on, that's the main thing on a night like tonight. There seem to have been quite a few fighters in the target area?"

"I'll say, Skipper!" This from Taffy, wiping his broken nose with his forearm. "I think Bob got a good shot at one as we left the target. Might have winged it. Weren't no flames. Silly sod flew right up alongside us, never saw us until Bob opened up."

"Thought he was going to fly straight into us, Skipper!" Bob Marshall said, his young face contorted into bafflement. You had a right to expect a night fighter pilot to be looking where he was going, especially over the target. Flying ops was dangerous enough without people – even the Luftwaffe - flying into you by accident. He went on, a little offended: "Mister Tilliard corkscrewed the kite so fast I couldn't really draw a bead on the fighter..."

"Make sure you put in a claim, Bob." Adam smiled. Putting two rows of tracers in front of a fellow's nose invariably persuaded him to go in search of a less wary target. "That's another 'possible' to go with that fellow you shot up over Berlin last month. Jolly good show!" He turned back to Tilliard. "You must have lost a good bit of altitude after you bumped into the fighter."

"Yes, sir. I assume we're one of the last back?"

"More or less. We're still waiting for B-Baker, K-King and Q-Queenie. Ben and the Adjutant are ringing around the emergency fields now. We should get some news soon."

Later, Adam slipped out of the Briefing Hall and walked briskly across to the watchtower. Although only half the crews had been debriefed so far he had formed a worrying picture of events over Germany. The marking had been scattered and the bombing effort had failed to achieve any real concentration. Another raid had gone off at half-cock. As many as ten heavies had gone down before the Main Force reached the target, possibly another dozen or so over Hanover.

"What's the gen?" He inquired brusquely, striding

into the Operations Room.

"B-Baker's down at Manston," Ben Hardiman reported, telephone in hand. "Had a run in with a fighter over the target. Bad news is the kite may be a write-off. Good news is the chaps are all in one piece. Well, barring a few bumps and bruises."

"That's something. Peter's brought the chaps back safe and sound, by the way. They bumped into a fighter. That's what held them up."

"A fighter?"

"It almost collided with them. Probably never saw them. Taffy reckons Bob winged it."

"Good for young Bob," grinned the big man.

"Mac's okay," Tom Villiers, the Adjutant called, putting his phone down. "K-King's *Gee* played up on the way back. They got lost and flew too close to Hull. Got shot up a bit but everybody's okay. Mac's put down at Pocklington. They'll have a look at K when it gets light. If she's not flyable we'll have to send a kite to pick up Mac and the others in the morning."

"What about Q-Queenie?"

"Nothing, sir. But we've still got some calls to make."

Adam propped himself against the corner of a desk, lit a cigarette and collected his wits. They ought to have heard something about Q by now. It was getting late. Q was either down somewhere safe or she was missing. Any kite still airborne would be flying with the fuel gauges reading EMPTY.

An hour later there was still no news of Q-Queenie.

She was gone.

Adam retired to his quarters for a nap at a little after seven. Already the eastern sky was lightening. Having spent the last twenty-four hours on his feet, sleep came easily with oblivion descending as his head touched the pillow. Notwithstanding, Crawford, his batman, would rouse him at nine. Crawford and he understood each other. The older man had listened with the utmost respectfulness as he had explained that he was a creature of habit.

'I don't sleep while my people are in the air. I like to make an early start on my in tray, ops permitting. Unless I've been flying the night before I expect you to wake me no later than oh-nine hundred hours irrespective of when I put my head down.'

The Squadron was stood down from operations at eleven that morning.

The leading edge of the latest cold front was rushing in from the Atlantic and it would strike the east coast bases of Bomber Command early that afternoon. By tonight the same weather front would be over northern Germany.

In the Mess somebody tuned into the mid-day news. According to the BBC, only 18 aircraft had failed to return from Hanover.

"B-Baker may not be a write-off after all, sir." Adam was able to tell Group Captain Alexander, encountering him in the corridor outside his office. "The starboard outer Merlin's had it, starboard undercarriage leg collapsed, but apart from that the kite's fairly sound. K-King will need a bit of patching up, probably a full maintenance, but she'll be back in the air by the end of the week."

The older man was a little preoccupied.

"Be a good chap, Adam. Think about taking a few days leave. While you can. If you won't take a few days leave then at least let Eleanor make a fuss of you. Oh, and that's an order, by the way!"

Chapter 23

Wednesday 20th October, 1943
St. Paul's Church, Ansham Wolds, Lincolnshire

They buried Barney's sprogs next to Q-Queenie's bomb-aimer. When Adam had explained the circumstances of the two men's deaths to the Reverend Naismith-Parry, the old man was horrified. He had refrained from mentioning that the dead bomb-aimer's replacement and the other six members of his old crew were now listed as 'missing'.

"Shot at by our own people?"

"Yes, sir. An unfortunate accident."

"Does this sort of thing happen often?"

"I'm afraid so, sir." Somebody, somewhere along the East Coast took a pot shot at Bomber Command's returning heavies most nights.

Today's turn out at the grave side was much reduced from the funeral of Q-Queenie's bomb-aimer, a little over a week ago. It was unavoidable given that the Squadron was readying itself for a major operation that night.

"The Squadron hasn't been stood down yet," Adam had remarked to the Rector, without elaborating. Many of the villagers who had attended the last burial had dutifully trooped up the hill to witness this service.

Eleanor approached Adam after the service.

"I'm sorry," she said, smiling apologetically. "I must rush back. I've left the children in the charge of Mrs Gray's eldest. Phoebe's a good girl, but I don't like to leave her to her own devices for any longer than absolutely necessary."

"Of course," he said, quickly. "It was good of you to come. These are miserable occasions."

"You're looking tired," Eleanor chided him, taking him aside out of earshot of the small party from the station. "Are you flying tonight?"

Adam met her eye.

"No." Had he planned to fly tonight he would surely have lied to her.

"I know I shouldn't ask. I'll try not to in future," she promised. "When shall I see you, next?"

"Tomorrow evening? Assuming nothing's on."

"All right. You need feeding up."

He hesitated. "About six? I should like to get to know Johnny and Emmy a little better. Last week you'd hidden them away by the time I arrived."

"That was because you were late," she admonished, very gently. Her brown eyes held him prisoner for a moment, released him reluctantly. "I'd like very much for you to get to know Johnny and Emmy better."

"Tomorrow, then." They squeezed hands and parted.

The battle order detailing the minutiae of the evening's entertainment was rattling off the Operations Room teleprinter as Adam shouldered his way through the Operations Room door. The massed Lancasters of 1, 5, 6 and 8 Groups were tasked to operate at maximum effort against Leipzig.

"Normal drill, I assume?" He checked cursorily, looking over the bombing leader's shoulder as he read out the preamble to the main orders.

"Cookie and maximum incendiaries. Take-off weights not to exceed sixty-three thousand pounds, sir."

"What do you reckon. Ten SBCs?"

"A dozen, possibly. I'll need to do some sums, sir. A dozen would probably be better. You get a better scatter from a dozen."

"A better scatter." Adam echoed, silently.

"Hello, everybody!" Ben Hardiman made his entrance, hung his greatcoat on the rack by the door. "Where's it to be tonight, chaps?"

"Leipzig."

The big man paused for thought, whistled. "Bloody Hell! That's miles away!"

"We're still waiting for details of the route."

Ben shrugged. Leipzig was ninety miles south-south-west of Berlin, the better part of six hundred miles from Ansham Wolds; an eight or nine hour round trip, perhaps longer. Good practice for the real thing, the Big City. The odds were the route would be straightforward, perhaps two or three long legs to minimise the mileage and to keep the ground track as tidy as possible. Operating at such long range the scope for innovation was negligible.

"Do we know what the latest met forecast's like?"

"Diabolical, old man."

"Oh. Nothing new there, then."

Adam walked across to the Readiness Board. Despite Q-Queenie's loss and the unserviceability of three other aircraft following the Hanover attack, the board was showing sixteen Lancasters ready for operations. Ben meanwhile was spreading maps of lower Saxony on the big ops table in the middle of the room.

"Thought so!" He announced, abruptly.

"What's that?" Adam asked, joining his friend.

"Look, here. See? The confluence of three rivers. The Elster, Pleisse and the Parther. At this time of year with the weather we've been seeing over Germany there should be lots of lovely reflective water slap bang in the middle of the city!"

There were knowing nods around the table. Even if Leipzig was hidden like Hanover beneath ten-tenths cloud, tonight the Pathfinders should, in theory, have a sporting chance of illuminating the target using *H2S* indications alone.

Adam detailed Barney Knight to conduct the main crew briefing that afternoon. As intended, the younger man – and everybody else - took it as a huge public vote of confidence after his run in with the Army.

'Look, sir,' his second-in-command had mumbled, awkwardly. 'I'm sorry about the other night, sir. I went a bit over the top. I gather you had to go out to bat on my behalf. Saved my bacon, and so on. It won't happen again.'

'Don't thank me, Barney,' Adam had retorted, coolly. 'Thank the Groupie. I'd hazard a guess Group Captain Alexander will be thinking of you tomorrow,' he went on, 'when he pays a call on Major-General Murchison at his Headquarters in York. The Deputy AOC has ordered him to partake of a large slice of humble pie on your behalf.'

'Oh, I see. Sorry, sir.'

Standing in front of the crews in the Briefing Hall, Barney radiated bulldog pugnacity. Although one of the sixteen aircraft listed as available for ops that morning had been scrubbed from the order of battle - due to a hydraulic failure – it still left fifteen crews to be briefed for the coming operation.

Faraway, Leipzig unknowingly awaited the pleasure of the Lancaster Force in the small hours of tomorrow morning. Each of the Squadron's heavies was loaded with a cookie and, after much discussion, twelve SBCs, each canister packed with up to ninety four-pound magnesium stick incendiaries.

"You will see that tonight's Aiming Point is situated just north of the centre of the main built-up area of the old city," Barney reminded the crews. As if they needed reminding. "In the heart of the *Altstadt.* In this part of the city most of the buildings date from the sixteenth and seventeenth century. The buildings are of predominantly wooden construction and the streets are narrow. Very narrow. This part of the city is a potential tinderbox. Even better, there are no natural firebreaks in this area of the city, so concentrated bombing in the vicinity of the AP will start a major conflagration. Hopefully, the sort of thing we've seen in the past in the Hanseatic ports of the north: Lubeck, Rostock, and of course, Hamburg."

Adam liked to think he would have said it with a

little less relish but the words could have been his own; Barney and he should have been blood brothers in this business not the strangers they had been until now. He sat on the stage, arms crossed, nodding implacable agreement while his second-in-command delivered an accomplished, polished performance.

"The forecast looks bad," Barney was saying. "We can't do anything about that. We'll just have to fly through it. There's no point belly-aching about it. We've just got to get on with it. Remember, if it is bad for us at twenty thousand feet think what it's like for the Jerries at ground level!"

Adam tried not to think about Leipzig, an ancient, beautiful city he had visited as a boy. Leipzig was a virgin target, a city with its heritage, factories, communications and defences intact, something that was becoming increasingly rare in Germany.

"When the Pathfinders turn east to start their run to the Initial Point, Eight Group's Mosquitoes will continue on to Berlin. With any luck the Jerries will get the wrong end of the stick and send the fighters to defend the Big City." Barney stood away from the lectern. "Hopefully, the Jerries will be caught with their pants down and we'll get a clear run in to Leipzig!"

Outside the Hall the Group Captain took Adam by the elbow.

"What do you think the odds are that the Chief will scrub tonight's op?"

"I think we'll go, sir."

"Looks fifty-fifty to me."

Adam decided not to argue the point. Tonight's operation would not be scrubbed. If the Main Force could strike a half-decent blow against a target as distant and dangerous as Leipzig on a night as filthy as this, it would send the enemy a chilling message. It would tell the defenders that there was nowhere in Germany Bomber Command could not find and wreck;

on any night, in any weather. The great mailed fist of the Main Force now hung like a fiery hammer above the cities of the German heartland and the Chief had no intention of letting the enemy forget it.

Not for a single minute.

Chapter 24

Wednesday 20th October, 1943
RAF Ansham Wolds, Lincolnshire

Suzy straightened her tunic, checked her hair one last time in the small, cracked mirror, and collected her faltering courage. She had made up her mind, made her decision. It was the biggest decision she had made in her young life.

Suzy had not yet told Peter Tilliard she had been put forward for a commission. She had not trusted herself to broach the subject even though she knew she owed it to him. It was as if deep down she understood that the decision had to be her own, and that it was unfair to ask the man to take responsibility for her.

Her guilt hung heavy.

She ought to have told him. Ought to have come straight out with it and opened her heart to him. Only, she was afraid to talk about it, terrified that by letting it out of the bag it would drive a wedge between them. That it would change things for ever and spoil everything.

It was cold and wet, and the mist clung to the ground as she walked out of the Waafery and headed purposefully towards the Flight Office. She tried to pretend that she had thought things through but in reality she had done no such thing. Until last night she had been in a hopeless dither, torn. Until last night she had convinced herself that she was grown up, in control, capable of retaining her dignity. Last night's events had swept away her illusions, cruelly mocking her girlish naivety.

Last night had been a nightmare.

She walked across the tarmac in a daze. The awfulness of waiting to find out if Peter was dead or alive had eroded her belief in things, and left her frightened, lonely, and somehow changed. Two erks on bicycles swerved to avoid her as she marched blindly into their path; they went on their way cursing softly and shaking their heads.

Suzy was oblivious, her world was closing in around her. If she turned down the chance of a commission she would probably stay a ranker for the duration, and never escape the motor pool. If she accepted the opportunity, new horizons would be open to her. Either way there was no guarantee she would remain at Ansham Wolds, in Lincolnshire, or even in England. It made it no easier to know, deep in her heart, that the choice was not really between carrying on as normal or letting her name go forward for a commission. There was no such thing as 'normal'. There was no safe option. She could stay at Ansham Wolds and Peter could be killed tomorrow, or she could leave Ansham Wolds and he could be killed tomorrow. Or he might live. The real choice was between passively carrying on and waiting to see if he was killed, or getting on with things and hoping for the best.

Last night's events had decided her upon the latter course of action.

She had to be practical and if that meant being a little cold-hearted, then she would have to be cold-hearted. At least with herself. She had absolutely no influence on whether Peter lived or died and she was not so naive as to pretend otherwise. No matter how awful it might seem to others, she had to look after herself. Love, and whatever time she and Peter had together was a bonus, literally a gift in the lap of the gods. So, she would accept things for what they were rather than what she wished them to be, and try as hard as she could to get on with the business of living.

Even now the guilt gnawed at her resolve.

The Senior WAAF looked her up and down, no doubt interpreting her diffidence as girlish shyness, attributing her hesitancy to childish modesty rather than the brutal quandaries of first love in a world gone mad.

"I take it you've made up your mind, then, Mills?" The Senior WAAF inquired, fixing Suzy with an intent, matronly scrutiny.

Suzy inadvertently bit her lower lip.

"Yes, Ma'am."

"Not before time."

"Yes, I'm sorry, Ma'am," Suzy stuttered, looking at her feet for a moment. "It was just that I thought it was best to think things over before I decided what to do."

"Most commendable."

Suzy took a deep breath.

"I'd very much like my name to go forward for a commission please, Ma'am."

Chapter 25

Thursday 21st October, 1943
Lancaster S-Sugar, 20 miles SSE of Leipzig

Two hundred and ten minutes out of Ansham Wolds the weariness fogged Peter Tilliard's mind. Most men reached the target half-frozen, fatigued and scared stiff. Such were the home truths the pilot of S-Sugar – flying the ninth op of his second Lancaster tour - took for granted. Twenty miles away the sky glowed as the Leipzig flak opened up. Searchlights played on the bottom of a swirling sea of clouds. Up ahead the openers ploughed on through the barrage by the twinkling light of falling Sky Markers.

There were at least three groups of markers.

"Shambles," he muttered to himself. "Jack, are you painting the target on your box of tricks, yet?" He called hopefully over the intercom.

"Yes, Skipper."

"Come up here and have a look. See if you can work out which Sky Markers we ought to be bombing!"

Jack Gordon was a self-confessed novice when it came to interpreting the image on the shimmering, flickering *H2S* screen. Although the screen was showing nothing remotely resembling the map of Leipzig before the off the navigation leader had foreseen just this eventuality. Mr and Mrs Gordon's first born might not be an *H2S* wizard, but Ben Hardiman was the real article, an out and out honest to god magician. No two ways about it. The proof of the pudding was that what Jack was now seeing on the small, blue-grey cathode ray tube corresponded almost exactly – albeit approximately, in a jagged, jittery, blurry sort of way - with what the Navigation Leader had predicted he would see approaching the city. S-Sugar was flying into the heart of a ragged circle of intense white returns set against a dark background. The blob of light sliding down the screen was Leipzig, the darkness around it the open countryside.

The Nav Leader had sketched a blackboard diagram of what he would see on the screen as they approached the target. His chalk had scratched noisily on the blackboard.

'Now then, chaps,' Ben had prefaced. 'What you're looking for is the confluence of the Elster and the Pleisse Rivers. There, in the southern suburbs of Leipzig. Identify that and the AP is about a mile or so to the north. All you have to do is get the confluence of the two rivers in the middle of the aiming circle on your screens and drop your bombs. With these ten centimetre sets that'll put your bomb loads down within a mile or so of the AP, whatever visibility you actually encounter over the target. If the Pathfinders cock up again tonight, the Wingco's keen that you bomb on *H2S* indications alone.'

Jack Gordon hesitated a moment, as if to double check he was actually seeing what he thought he was seeing on the small, pulsing cathode ray screen of the bomber's downward looking radar.

"Not necessary, Skipper!" He reported, confidently. "I've got the IP on the tube. If you've got ten-tenths up ahead we can bomb blind."

Tilliard flicked his intercom switch.

"Pilot to navigator. There are markers going down all over the shop up ahead. Just like the other night. We'll bomb on your word. Pilot to bomb-aimer."

"Bomb-aimer to pilot."

"We'll bomb on the navigator's command, Round Again."

"Roger, Skipper!"

The infernal glow of the screen lit Jack Gordon's face. Over Hanover two nights before the screen had been filled with returns from the city, the familiar white out effect had made it useless as a blind bombing tool.

Not so tonight. The Elster and the Pleisse Rivers, swollen by the autumn rains, shone like faint silvery threads, beckoning S-Sugar from afar.

"Come right five degrees, Skipper!" Then: "Five minutes to run."

Tilliard felt the presence of Ted Hallowes at his shoulder.

The engineer had wedged himself behind the pilot's seat and was scanning the sky for danger. Although there were no fighters the flak was rising through the clouds in tight, radar-predicted boxes all across the city. Unexpectedly strong following winds had scattered the bomber stream, nullified *Window*, and given the gunners real radar targets - rather than shadows - to shoot at. A mile to port a heavy exploded in the night, showering flames as it tumbled earthwards. From four miles below the blast waves of cookies striking ground in the open fields and woods east and south of the city began to reach up into the night, shaking the clouds.

Jack Gordon concentrated on the flickering cathode ray tube – which was barely the circumference of his open hand - on his desk. He watched patiently as the confluence of the Elster and Pleisse Rivers slid down into the aiming ring. He took a long, deep breath. Sucked in oxygen, tried to ignore the chaffing of his mask.

"Navigator to bomb-aimer. Prepare to drop bombs."

"Bomb-aimer to navigator, roger."

Somewhere in the white out of ground returns north of the two rivers lay the tinder-dry, closely packed wooden heart of the old town, the *Altstadt*.

"Now, Round Again! Drop the bombs NOW!"

S-Sugar soared as the two-ton cookie and more than a thousand stick incendiaries dropped from her cavernous bomb bay. Immediately, Tilliard put the bomber's nose down into a shallow drive and pushed the throttles up against the stops. The sky was full of Lancasters and hundreds of bomb loads were falling randomly across a huge swathe of southern Saxony.

"Bomb bay doors...SHUT!" Reported the flight engineer, resuming his watching brief at his pilot's shoulder. In the distance a streamer of flame fell into the seething, boiling clouds as another heavy died.

"Pilot to navigator. Make sure you draw the Wingco a picture of that AP, Jack."

"What do you think I'm doing now, Skipper!" Jack shouted back, laughing.

Tilliard smiled to himself before turning his thoughts to the trip back. Tonight, getting home involved the small matter of a five hour flight across occupied Europe, fighting strong head winds all the way.

It was going to be a long, tedious slog.

Chapter 26

Thursday 21st October, 1943
RAF Ansham Wolds, Lincolnshire

Adam was alone in his office drinking brandy-laced cocoa. The openers would be over Leipzig about now. Cookies would be smashing whole neighbourhoods, tens of thousands of incendiaries would be tumbling, scattering down into the wreckage.

He hoped Peter Tilliard was taking good care of his crew. The chaps had said very little about the Hanover op. A good sign. Confirmation if confirmation was required that his assessment of Peter's flying skills had been spot on. The chaps would have had plenty to say if they had identified any question marks. He planned to reclaim his crew for the next big raid. Assuming that was, the next big one was to somewhere interesting; a target where the Main Force was doing more than just turning the rubble. He had sat out too many shows lately and it was time to get back into the saddle. High time.

The Senior WAAF's *Fraternisation* report sat malignantly on his blotter like an unexploded bomb with a ticking time-delay fuse. Either Squadron Officer Laing had a very dirty mind or the station was a den of iniquity, Sodom and Gomorrah authentically reincarnated on the Lincolnshire Wold.

The Senior WAAF wanted him to make an example of somebody and nothing short of a public crucifixion would satisfy her. He was deeply disappointed with Squadron Officer Laing. He had a right to expect her *not* to drop *her* dirty linen, willy-nilly, on his plate. If she wanted to embark on a moral crusade *she* ought to have joined the Salvation Army.

He sighed, dug out a cigarette.

Sky Markers would be drifting down over Leipzig:

iridescent white and red fires in the sky blowing on the wind, floating, swaying beneath their parachutes. Ten, twenty Sky Markers, perhaps more lighting the night, calling the openers in to attack. The sky over Leipzig would be filled with the rumbling thunder of hundreds of Merlins. For the men, women and children in the shelters the ordeal was only just beginning...

He determined to have one last talk with Squadron Officer Laing, to try to persuade her to tone down her report, and preferably withdraw it. One last chat to try to get her to understand that there was a war going on. He would demand concrete evidence of the misdemeanours she claimed were commonplace. Pointedly ask her for a little less tittle-tattle and a few more facts. Chapter and verse. He would seize the initiative, force her onto the back foot.

It might do some good but he was not very optimistic.

He could and would have requested her re-assignment away from Ansham Wolds if he honestly believed her machinations were actually detrimental to the morale of his crews. He had culled four section heads since he arrived at Ansham Wolds. Those men had been dead wood, not up to the job. Squadron Officer Laing on the other hand was undeniably efficient, self-evidently devoted to *her girls* and if only she had not got this bee in her bonnet over the fraternisation issue, they might have coexisted in perfect harmony. The last thing he wanted to do right now was lose another section head. The last thing he wanted was to have *his* key section heads constantly looking over their shoulders.

Tom Villiers had, on his behalf, spelled this out to the woman.

'She means well, sir.' He had concluded resignedly. 'The WAAFs on this station need somebody who is both conscientious and dare I say it, protective. Many of the girls are away from home for the first times in their lives.

Some of them are very young, Squadron Officer Laing is simply a tad overzealous at times...'

Adam dropped the report into his desk draw and locked it away. If the Group Captain got hold of it Barney Knight would be for the high jump. No two ways about it. He planned to speak to his second-in-command on his return from Leipzig and caution him to keep his nose clean. It was no bad thing that the Old Man planned to be off the station tomorrow.

He lit his cigarette, inhaled wearily. His cocoa was getting cold.

The showdown with the Senior WAAF came, unexpectedly, at four o'clock in the morning in the Briefing Hall. She could not possibly have chosen a worst time or place to seek a showdown. In the background the Intelligence Officer was readying his debriefers to greet the crews on their return from Leipzig when Squadron Officer Laing bustled up to Adam, interrupting his conversation with the Adjutant. She was adamant. She said she wanted action. She had been led to believe that action would be forthcoming and she demanded it sooner rather than later. Tom Villiers had turned his gaze to the ceiling, rolled his eyes, and audibly groaned in despair.

"I trust you're not thinking of reneging on your undertaking of last week, Wing-Commander?" The woman asked, digging in her heels.

Adam had stuck to the rules, Marquis of Queensberry rules, and got nowhere. Now it was time to take the gloves off.

"Squadron Officer Laing," he growled, getting to his feet. "You and I clearly have different priorities. I'm fighting the Germans. You on the other hand, seem to be more interested in fighting me."

The Senior WAAF's face suddenly wore a startled look.

"I've read your report," he continued. "Frankly, I'm

not interested in barrack room gossip, and I'm more than a little disappointed that you should have formed the impression that I am. However, since you seem so preoccupied with maintaining discipline, I suggest that in future you address your efforts towards the restoration of good order among the women under your command. If your report is to be believed this is obviously an area you have been neglecting of late. If you have evidence, and I mean proper evidence, that breaches of regulations have occurred then kindly employ the appropriate channels to prosecute those infractions. And stop wasting my bloody time!"

"Really, Wing-Commander!" The woman blurted, her cheeks colouring. "I must protest..."

Adam cut her off in mid-stream.

"Should you choose to forward your report to the Station Commander, you will not receive my support. In fact I shall fight you every inch of the way. I trust we understand each other?"

Adam stalked back to his quarters, roused Rufus and went for a brisk walk to restore his equilibrium before the returning crews landed. The Senior WAAF had a decision to make. Either she put up or shut up. She was either on his side or she was not. If the answer was *not*, then there was no place for her at Ansham Wolds.

His crews were at Ansham Wolds to fly *his* heavies to Germany; providing they did that to *his* satisfaction they were entitled a certain leeway. He liked to run a tight ship, but nobody was going to undermine the morale of *his* people. Nobody. He was the last man to turn a blind eye to overt fraternization on the station but what a man did off-station was, all things being equal, his own affair. Assuming a chap ensured a liaison did not adversely affect his performance on ops; who was he to meddle?

"Wing-Commander!"

Adam shut his eyes, stopped in his tracks. The

bloody woman was dogging his every step! The Senior WAAF scurried towards him, puffing heavily.

"I felt I had to speak to you, sir," she gasped, catching up with him.

He set off again, at a reduced pace.

"Oh." Rufus sniffed around the newcomer.

"In case there had been a, er, misunderstanding. When we spoke earlier?"

Adam's ear caught the distant rumble of Merlins in the south. He said nothing.

"I'm dreadfully sorry if you feel I'm not pulling my weight, sir," Squadron Officer Laing said, worriedly. "I'd like to assure you that my priorities are the same as your own. And I'm sorry if anything I've done has given rise to offence. Truly sorry."

This took the wind out of Adam's sails.

"Look," he said, "what I said back in the Hall. It was a tad unfair." He halted to light a cigarette and to give the woman a chance to recover her breath. There were more Merlins in the southern sky, now. The Main Force was running for home ahead of the dawn, fleeing before the new day.

"With respect, I disagree, sir. I got off on the wrong foot with Wing-Commander Fulshawe, too," the woman confessed. "It was my fault. Bull in a china shop, and all that. Always been like it, I'm afraid. My request for a transfer to another Station will be on the Group Captain's desk later this morning, sir."

"No, no," Adam objected, half-heartedly. "I won't have that."

There were several Lancasters circling over Ansham Wolds. The flare path lamps started to blink on in the distance. More aircraft were joining the circuit every minute. The night was alive with Merlins.

"I feel it's for the best, sir."

A red flare shot across the blackness high overhead. *Wounded onboard.*

The Senior WAAF slipped away into the darkness, realising that she was intruding and that she no longer belonged. Adam watched the red flare slowly arcing down to the ground. When he looked around again, Squadron Officer Laing was gone.

In the morning Adam sought out Barney Knight and discovered him ruefully inspecting B-Baker in front of the hangars. The outer half of the Lancaster's port wing was pocked with ragged holes. Some of the holes were large enough for a man to put his fist in. 100-Octane fuel still dripped from the punctured wing tanks into piles of sand and sawdust.

"Strayed a tad too far south coming back," the younger man reported. "Got a bit of a working over from the Frankfurt flak. Could have been worse."

"How's your nav?"

"He won't be sitting down for a while, sir." B-Baker's navigator had suffered ugly, thankfully superficial shrapnel wounds to his buttocks and legs. Although other aircraft had returned bearing minor flak marks, mercifully, he was the Squadron's only casualty. Barney grinned roguishly. "Serves him right, getting us lost like that! Look what the bastards did to my kite!"

Adam thought he was being a little harsh on the lad.

"We need to have a chat," he said, abruptly. "In private." He led Knight around the Lancaster, up into the fuselage and through to the cockpit. Leaning against the back of the pilot's seat he viewed the other man unsmiling. "Can I take it as read that you're the Secretary of the local Lancaster Heaven Club?"

"Er, I'm not sure I know what you mean, sir?" Barney said, more in hope than conviction.

"No?" Foremost among the Senior WAAF's complaints was the allegation that several of her young ladies had been 'joyriding' in his Lancasters. This was a common enough pastime, but a pastime which could not have continued for any length of time without the tacit acquiescence of one or both of Adam's Flight Commanders. Mac would never have had truck with this kind of nonsense, it was more in Barney's line. "Never mind. Perhaps, you could give him, whoever he is, a message from me?"

"Of course, sir. Anything I can do to help, sir."

Adam's grim visage cracked a little.

"Let him know that I'm not terribly keen about unauthorised personnel flying in my Lancs. Nothing personal, but I don't approve of the misuse of Government property in general, and I particularly disapprove of it when the items in question are WAAFs."

"Yes, sir."

"Call me old-fashioned," Adam went on. "But I suspect that if the Almighty in His infinite wisdom had intended chaps to court young ladies at five thousand feet he'd probably have modified our equipment in more ways than one. Quite apart from giving us wings."

Barney nodded thoughtfully, wisely keeping his mouth firmly shut.

"So," Adam concluded. "If you could put the word out that if the chaps must misuse WAAFs, they're not to do it anywhere near my Lancs, I'd be obliged."

"I'll do my best, sir."

"Or, for that matter, anywhere near the Senior WAAF"

"Well away from the Senior WAAF, sir," echoed the younger man, recognising at last that the Wingco was struggling to keep a straight face. In the light of his recent contretemps with General Murchison, and now this, Barney was finding it impossible to regard Adam Chantrey as the humourless interloper he had once seemed.

"Whoever she may be," Adam added, ironically.

Barney stared at him, blankly. Squadron officer Laing was an Ansham Wolds institution, more firmly rooted in the earth of the high wold than the

Brandenburg Gate was in Berlin.

"Why, is the Senior WAAF likely to be moving on then, sir?"

The stench of leaking petrol hung in the air.

"Let's get out of here," Adam decided. He needed a smoke. "She and I had a heart to heart last night," he explained as they walked away from B-Baker. "A meeting of minds, as it were. I believe she's considering her position."

Chapter 27

Thursday 21st October, 1943
Ansham Wolds, Lincolnshire

Suzy walked around the old, battered Austin in the dusk. The tiny little car with its dented running boards and peeling paintwork was much, much more than a car to her, it was adventure. A new departure. The car had drawn alongside as she was walking down the hill to the village, a rendezvous having been arranged outside the Sherwood Arms. Peter Tilliard cranked up the handbrake, pushed open the passenger door.

"Hop in, sharpish!" He urged her. "Somebody's bound to come along."

Suzy slammed the door shut behind her, leaned over to the man, her mouth finding his.

"Why didn't you tell me?" She exclaimed, brightly. "Whose car is this?"

"Jack Gordon's," he grinned, crashing home first gear and letting the Austin roll forward. "He sort of inherited it. As you do. I didn't tell you about it before because we didn't have any petrol for it."

Suzy knew better than to ask him where he had got hold of petrol. 'Requisitioning' 100-octane for private use was a court-martial offence regardless of the fact most old lags considered it a perk of operational flying. A perk on a par with walking around the station with the top button of their tunics undone. She also knew better than to inquire further how the car had come into Jack Gordon's hands. When aircrew talked about 'inheriting' a thing, it usually meant that the *thing's* previous owner was missing or dead. She had yet to meet Jack Gordon but the Australian's hard-drinking, hard-playing reputation went before him. He and Peter seemed to have hit it off, become firm friends in no time. Unlikely friends. Peter was so quiet, sensible, normal. The opposite of just about everything she had heard about his new navigator.

"Where are you taking me? Are we still going to Scunthorpe?"

"I thought we might go somewhere a bit quieter. You know, where we're not likely to bump into anybody we need to worry about from the station. Jack recommended a couple of places where we'd be among friends."

"Did he!" Suzy exclaimed, suddenly feeling unaccountably threatened.

"Look," Tilliard replied, reacting to the shrill edge in her voice. "All the chaps know about us. The crew, anyway. Jack was just trying to be helpful, that's all."

The woman stared into the dark countryside bumping, jolting past the window. She resented the idea that he had been talking about them to somebody else. To strangers, especially to Jack Gordon, A Flight's notorious chief prankster.

"We can trust the chaps to keep mum," Tilliard promised, misreading her mood and misconstruing her fears.

"Can we?"

He drove through Ansham Wolds, out of the village. The lane narrowed to little more than a track as it meandered east. It was dark when he parked at the bottom of the hill in Kingston Magna, outside the blacked out *Hare and Hounds*.

Kingston Magna remained largely untouched by the upheavals the RAF had visited on neighbouring Ansham Wolds. It was that little bit farther from the airfield, that little bit harder to get to, half-hidden in the landscape and somewhat off the well-travelled roads that all now pointed to Ansham Wolds.

"I thought it would be nice to go somewhere quiet, that's all," Tilliard said, patiently. "Jack knows the lie of the land hereabouts much better than I do. I asked him if he could recommend anywhere. All right?"

The anger blazed in Suzy's eyes. Nameless, blind anger. Nothing had prepared her for the terror that had crept up upon her on that night of the Hanover raid. At first she had been proud, so proud to wave Peter off to war. Then after the last of the Squadron's Lancasters had disappeared into the night the dreadful, aching emptiness had filled her like ice, freezing deep and hard in her soul. Later, when the other aircraft landed and there was no sign of S-Sugar, the terror had turned into despair, a hopeless desolation, a nightmare. She had hung around the Briefing Hall, fetching and carrying trays of cocoa, waiting, waiting until she had given up hope, begun to reconcile herself with the certainty that the man she adored was dead.

'There's another Lanc in the circuit,' somebody had called. The minutes had ticked by: one, two, three, four... Each minute was an eternity. She had shrunk into the shadows, wanted to burst into floods of tears, longed to curl up in a heap on the nearest chair.

Then the nightmare had evaporated.

'B-Beer, everybody! Good old Tilly, he's brought the Wingco's crew back!'

Seeing Peter shuffling into the Hall, blinking in the bright light, she had wanted to throw herself into his arms. Instead she had played her part, kept up her pretence and outwardly at least, retained her dignity.

She had gone through it all again last night.

It was so unfair.

Suzy wanted to be hugged, cuddled, comforted yet in that moment something snapped and to her horror, she found herself rounding on the man. Lashing out. Blindly, bitterly as the terrors of recent nights resurfaced.

"So what exactly did Jack recommend? Take her out into the middle of nowhere to some horrid little back room and try your luck with her?"

Tilliard stared at her wide-eyed. Suzy glared back at him wildly. In a moment she had pushed open the passenger door, and was running away from the car. Dumbstruck, for a moment the man watched her go.

Do something!

Do something you clot!

He leapt out and ran after the woman, his feet splashing in the mud the afternoon's rain had washed out of the hedgerows.

"Suzy!" He cried, his long legs devoured the ground between them. He caught up with her around the corner. "It's not like that!" He protested, grabbing her arm. "It's not like that at all!" Instantly, she fell into his arms, she buried her face in his chest, sobbing breathlessly, clinging to him. The man held her tight. "Really and truly," he muttered in her ear. "I had no intention of luring you into some horrid little room, or of trying my luck with you. Honestly, Suzy. I just thought it would be nice to be together. Have a drink, talk. That's all. You know, away from things. Safe."

She sniffed, slipped from his embrace, and wiped away her tears with the crumpled handkerchief he handed her. Presently she found her voice.

"Let's go in. Before it starts raining, again."

She took his hand, leaned on him as they walked back down the lane.

Their entrance elicited a number of raised, curious eyebrows from the handful of regulars propping up the bar of the *Hare and Hounds* so soon after opening time. By mid-evening the inn would be crowded with A Flight's old lags.

"Hello, there," Tilliard grimaced at the Publican. The man was a dead-ringer for his opposite number at the Sherwood Arms in Ansham Wolds, four miles up the road. "My navigator recommended your best ale, landlord," he added, remembering Jack's advice.

"Ah, you'll be a friend of Mr. Gordon's then?"

"Er, his pilot, yes." Tilliard ordered a pint of bitter for himself, a half for Suzy who hovered uneasily behind his shoulder.

The Landlord refused to accept his money.

"House rule, sir," he explained, beaming. "The landlord reserves the right to stand any friend of Jack Gordon's a round. Every now and again, leastways. My name's Bill Bowman, my brother Arnold has the Sherwood Arms. You and your young lady are always welcome here, sir."

"Why, that's awfully decent of you. Er, Bill. I'm Peter Tilliard," he returned, shaking the Publican's big, calloused hand. "And this is Suzy."

The woman stepped out of his shadow. She manufactured a smile.

"How do you do."

"There's a nice warm fire in the snug," the ruddy-faced landlord said, "through the door over there. You make yourselves at home. Nobody will trouble you in there. I'll see to that."

The *Hare and Hounds* was an old coaching inn. Gnarled oak beams held up the low ceiling and a glowing fire burned in the big, red brick hearth. The floor was uneven, and the rough-hewn wooden furniture rickety.

"I really didn't expect to be made quite so welcome," Tilliard whispered when the couple were alone in the room.

"Peter," Suzy sniffed. "What I said. Forget I ever said it. I didn't mean it, any of it. Really, I didn't." Her blue eyes settled on his face, imploring him to understand. "It's just that I've been so worried. When you were flying I couldn't bear it. I'm sorry, I shouldn't tell you this, I know you've got enough on your plate as it is."

He moved closer, touched her knee.

"It's all right. When we were last back from Hanover it must have been horrible?"

She nodded, close to tears.

"I didn't think it would be like this."

"I'm sorry."

They held hands.

"I thought we'd have more time," Suzy said, the twinkle returning in her eyes when she met his gaze. "I suppose the thing is to make the best of things? Isn't that what they say?"

"Yes."

"So that's what we shall do," she declared. "I'll try not to be silly again, I promise." He was about to tell her that she could go ahead and be as silly as she wanted to be whenever the mood took her. "And there's something I have to tell you," Suzy went on, before he could speak. "I've been put forward for a commission."

"A commission?"

"Yes." She smiled nervily.

"Why, that's tremendous news. Wizard news!"

"You mean you don't mind?"

"Mind? Of course not!" He exclaimed. "Have you written to your people about it? They'll be dead chuffed, I shouldn't wonder!"

Suzy shook her head.

"No, I haven't told anybody about it yet."

"Why ever not? It really is wizard news!"

"You don't mind? You really don't mind?"

"Of course I don't mind. When did you find out?" Tilliard asked, basking in the heat from the fire and his pleasure in hearing Suzy's good news.

"Last week. I didn't know what to do. I was afraid to tell you."

"Silly, girl," he chided, gently.

"I know that now!" Suddenly, everything seemed so simple and Suzy felt very, very foolish.

"Have they given you a date for your course?"

"I'm to report to the depot at Shrewsbury at oh-nine hundred hours the Monday after next. It's a thirty-day initial assessment and training course. If I pass I get a seven day leave, and then they can post me anywhere."

"Monday week," he mused. "That soon?" It was for the best. The last thing he wanted was Suzy worrying herself to death every time he was in the air. This way she would never know when he was flying. There were times to try to be romantic and there were times to be practical. This was one of the latter. There was no point pretending things were anything other than what they were, unknown and unknowable, like his future.

"Will you write to me?" She inquired, being brave.

"Every day."

"Promise?"

"Scout's honour," he vowed, sipping his beer.

Driving slowly back to the station Suzy rested her head on the man's shoulder.

"Can we pull over, darling?"

"We're a bit late, I don't want you to get into any trouble."

"I don't care."

He stopped the car on the verge, engine idling noisily. They kissed, held each other.

"Before I leave for Shrewsbury," Suzy informed him. "I expect you to take advantage of me. In fact, if you don't, I shall never, ever forgive you. A horrid little back room in the middle of nowhere would do very nicely, thank you." The words spilled out of her mouth in a rush.

The man was at a loss. He was perfectly content to settle for being with Suzy when he could, for embraces snatched in the shadows, the occasional touch of her lips on his. She had given him a renewed hope and belief in the rightness of things and he had expected nothing from her in return, or in his schoolboy innocence imagined there would be more. Not while he was on ops, not while the war went on. Taking advantage of her had been, and remained farthest from his mind. He wanted to be her protector from evil and initially, he was a little shocked by what she was suggesting. She was soft and warm in his arms and the scent of her blond hair made his senses reel.

"Look, you deserve a chap who can take care of you," he objected, lamely. "Not a chap like me."

Her mouth pressed against his, moistly, hotly.

"But I love you, silly."

Chapter 28

Friday 22nd October, 1943
Ansham Wolds, Lincolnshire

Eleanor opened the door of the cottage to be confronted by her father's smug smile. Although, she had not expected Adam to call that evening the knock at the door had suddenly raised her hopes and she was unable to completely veil her disappointment.

"Father?" She heard the car driving away up the hill.

"Eleanor, my dear," he smiled, stepping into the hallway, planting a cursory kiss on her cheek. "This is just a flying visit. I've got an appointment at Bawtry Hall tomorrow."

The woman picked up his big, heavy Gladstone bag, and hauled it inside. The old man wandered into the parlour, looking thin, ashen and very fragile. He dumped himself wearily in the chair in front of the fire.

"You're staying the night?"

"Yes, my dear," he sighed, betraying a profound weariness. "My driver will collect me bright and early tomorrow morning. I'll go straight back down to London when my business at Bawtry Hall is concluded. I'm not putting you out at all, am I?"

Eleanor was assailed by a pang of guilt.

"No, of course not. It's lovely to see you again so soon. It's just that I was a bit surprised to find you on the doorstep, that's all."

"You weren't expecting anybody else, then?"

"Goodness, no! Who on earth would I be expecting at this time of day?"

"I don't know."

She frowned. "I shall make a pot of tea."

"Capital idea."

Eleanor fled to the kitchen. At this hour last night

she had been in Adam's arms. He had been late, desperately apologetic, upset to have missed the children whom she had long since put to bed. 'Shut up,' she had said, kissing him until he did. They had eaten dinner, settled in front of the fire. She had doused the lamps, draped herself across his lap in the warm darkness, safe from all evil in his embrace. It was like being a girl again; everything was tingling new, fresh and exciting.

'I've put up a bit of a black with the Groupie,' Adam had confessed, stroking Eleanor's hair. 'There was a frightful stink after the Army shot up our sprogs on Sunday night and Barney got a bit carried away. Not that he didn't have every right to, of course. Anyway, the long and the short of it was the Groupie was in York today pouring oil on troubled waters. Then when he got back he discovered the Senior WAAF had put in a transfer request. Needless to say he wasn't a happy man!'

'Group Captain Alexander has always struck me as being a very kind man,' Eleanor had observed, distractedly. 'A perfect gentleman.'

'Martinet with a heart of gold,' Adam had retorted, planting a kiss in her hair. They had talked more about his childhood, especially his summers in Germany. She had teased him about Inge, his 'first love'. Despite his tongue-in-cheek protestations that Inge had broken his heart it seemed they had remained on good terms, corresponded cordially, regularly with each other right up until the outbreak of war. Inge had married another childhood friend, a Luftwaffe pilot, Hans Joachim Bruckner, the son of a senior Wehrmacht officer. Adam had travelled to Germany to attend their wedding in Berlin in the spring of 1939. There was respect, even a hint of admiration in his voice when he spoke about his 'rival'.

'What was he like?' Eleanor had prompted, softly.

'Confident, cocky, laughing eyes. Typical single-engine fighter sort,' he told her. 'Barney Knight's a dead-ringer for him. They could be brothers.'

Something warned Eleanor not to pursue the subject, so she had steered the conversation onto other matters and thought her own thoughts. Adam admitted to no other woman in his life since Inge in his mid-teens. He was entitled to his secrets, as she was to hers. Since he was self-evidently a man who enjoyed the company of women, she assumed there must have been other women, possibly several, in his life. No matter...

'I often think about my mother's people in Austria,' she said. 'You know, wondering what's become of them. You hear such awful things. It must be the same for you? With your German friends?'

'No, not really. Everything's changed. I've changed, they'll have changed. The ones who are still alive, anyway. Besides,' he had laughed, ruefully, 'Inge broke my heart, remember?'

'I shall never forget it!'

For a brief moment Eleanor had been sorely tempted to confide to him that she was about to be hauled in front of the local Magistrate for yet another, alleged, most likely wholly spurious infringement of the blackout regulations. She was convinced now that Edward Rowbotham, the village's Chief ARP Warden was conducting some kind of personal vendetta against her. Having checked and rechecked the cottage's blackout, spent hours relining, refitting panels, rehanging drapes, not a single flicker of light could possibly escape from the Gatekeeper's Lodge. The charges were so petty, so mean. Even if the stupid little man had had some kind of grudge against Harry's people, it was nothing to do with her. She had ached to pour out her heart to Adam. And yet in a funny sort of way she was immensely proud that she had not. He would have been very angry and would have felt obliged to intervene; he had quite enough on his plate without the added distraction of her silly little problems.

Eleanor had recovered her equilibrium by the time she rejoined her father in the parlour. She laid the tea tray on the floor by the fire, knelt by the hearth and poured the tea.

"You look different," the old man remarked.

"Nonsense!"

"No. You look years younger, my dear."

"It's your imagination."

Her father raised an eyebrow, unsteadily took the cup and saucer she held out. He knew he was not mistaken. Eleanor was different, changed and the disappointment in his daughter's face when she opened the door had been palpable. Her brown eyes sparkled, there was a new colour in her cheeks and for the first time since her husband had gone overseas, she had taken a great deal of care with her hair. And was that a suggestion of rouge on her cheeks?

"Have you seen anything of the dashing Wing-Commander, lately?" He asked, affecting innocence but with a mischievous glint in his rheumy gaze. His daughter's irritation instantly confirmed everything he needed to know.

"As it happens, yes." Eleanor said brusquely. "If you'll excuse me I'll make up the spare bed."

So that was it! The old man stared wistfully into his tea leaves as he listened to his daughter moving about upstairs. Eleanor reminded him so much of her mother, his beloved Hannah. She was so independent, so fearless, so breathtakingly, darkly beautiful. He had never understood what Eleanor saw in Harry Grafton. A pleasant enough fellow and for all his shortcomings decent to the core, but hardly a man who was ever going to amount to anything. Now his little girl had been swept off her feet by of all people, Adam Chantrey.

Life was full of surprises.

Faraway, 647 Squadron's Lancasters were taking off.

One after another they roared into the air and climbed into the night. The window panes rattled softly as the massed Merlins of the Main Force sang on high and sent their deep, throaty roar tumbling down to earth.

Bomber Command was going to war.

Eleanor came downstairs, sat with her father by the fire.

"It's funny how Johnny and Emmy sleep through this?"

"Children can get used to almost anything."

The old man became aware that his daughter's eyes were fixed on him.

"I hope they never get used to this," she said with a quiet, passionate vehemence.

Chapter 29

Saturday 23rd October, 1943
Lancaster O-Orange, 15 miles North of Kassel

The city was burning. The clouds that had saved Hanover and Leipzig earlier in the week had forsaken Kassel. Beneath a clear, starry sky the Pathfinders had laid their red spot markers in the heart of the city; and despite the presence of a large number of night fighters over the target the Main Force had pressed home its attack with unusual precision and persistence. The fires had taken hold within minutes and now as O-Orange flew away from the target flames lit the southern horizon.

Nobody said much.

No old lag crowed over the death of a city and besides, the road to Kassel had been signposted by the wrecks of burning heavies. There would be missing faces in the Mess in the morning. Many, many missing faces. It had been a bloody night's work and it was not over yet.

"Pilot to gunners," Adam drawled laconically over the static hiss of the intercom. "No fire-watching, chaps. Keep your eyes peeled for bandits. The bad guys won't all have gone home."

The conflagration illuminated a Halifax flying a thousand feet below. The Halifaxes would have had a bad night tonight. As soon as the fighters got into the bomber stream a large number of Lancaster pilots would have clawed for height, regardless of orders, an option unavailable to the crews of the Halifaxes.

Adam was not often rattled but tonight there had been several moments when he was seriously discommoded. The fighters had swarmed over Kassel, dived into the flak and hacked down countless heavies. He had never seen so many fighters over a target, circling like sharks as wave after wave of heavies relentlessly washed over the burning city.

"Flamer astern at four o'clock!" Taffy reported. "Didn't see any tracer but there was no flak. Put it down to a fighter!"

Ben acknowledged the report without comment. Noting the time and position in his log he eased himself to his feet, stood up in the astrodome at the rear of the cockpit. He stretched his legs, stared back at the inferno engulfing Kassel.

"Bloody Hell," he muttered, forgetting the intercom channel was open. It seemed as if the whole southern sky was on fire. Mile upon mile of Kassel was burning. "Looks like we've got a result tonight, chaps," he whistled.

It was symptomatic of how close Adam was to the end of his tether that he very nearly bawled out his friend for his inadvertent misuse of the intercom.

"Pilot to navigator," he inquired, tersely. "How far to the next turning point, please?"

"Approximately eight minutes, Skipper."

"Roger."

Ted Hallowes patted Adam's shoulder.

"Number four's running hot, Skipper." He shouted, briefly removing his oxygen mask. "Can we come down on the revs?"

Something substantial had struck the aircraft just before they bombed. Adam had felt the impact through the controls. It was as if the Lancaster had hit a deep pothole taxiing. The flak over Kassel was desultory. Adam had wondered, for a split second – and then forgotten all about it – if O-Orange had been hit by a falling incendiary, perhaps several. A lot of pilots would have pulled out all the stops and climbed as high as possible on a night like this. Not that it mattered, there would be plenty of time to examine the kite properly when they got home.

Throttling back the over-heating Merlin did not solve

the problem.   Sixty miles north of Kassel the decision was taken to feather the engine.

"Pilot to crew," Adam announced, phlegmatically. "We've got a problem with number four.   Stand by for feathering.   Out."

He made a thumbs up signal to the flight engineer.

"Master fuel cock...OFF!"

"Button in...RELEASE BUTTON!"

"Throttle...CLOSED!"

"Slow-running cut-out switch...SET TO IDLE CUT-OFF POSITION!"

Hallowes craned his neck, checked the Merlin had actually stopped, and confirmed that the propeller was feathered, wind milling in the slipstream.

"Number four FEATHERED!"

Adam adjusted the throttles to maintain airspeed and altitude on the three remaining engines.   Relieved of her bomb load O-Orange should handle happily enough on three sound Merlins.   Assuming nothing else broke there was no cause for undue alarm.   He scanned his instruments, searching for the minutest irregularity, the first hint of another problem.   Hallowes was doing the same with his dials.

"Pilot's controls seem okay.   What about your board, Ted?"

"All okay, Skipper."

"Pilot to crew.   We must have picked up some damage over the target.   Everybody double check your stations for damage."   Adam breathed a sigh of relief when the last report came in.   The feathered Merlin apart, O-Orange appeared to be in one piece.   "Pilot to crew," he acknowledged, "All the dials are okay up here and from the way the kite's flying all the control surfaces must be intact."   He always made a point of giving the chaps the good news as well as the bad.   "We'll be back a little later than planned on three engines.   Pilot out."

"Navigator to pilot.   Turning point in one minute.

Prepare to alter left to two-eight-zero on my mark."

"Turn left to two-eight-zero on your mark. Roger."

The intercom hissed.

"Turn left onto two-eight-zero...NOW!"

Chapter 30

Saturday 23rd October, 1943
RAF Ansham Wolds, Lincolnshire

In the morning the squadrons counted the cost. Adam found Mac grimly surveying the mauled flanks of his beloved K-King, the gallant old warhorse in which he had flown seventeen of his twenty-one ops.

"Fighter?" Adam murmured, shivering in the wintery breeze.

Mac shrugged.

"Probably, sir," he replied, staring morosely at the ragged gashes in the Lancaster's after fuselage. "Nobody saw anything. There wasn't a lot of flak."

The starboard rudder and elevator assembly was in tatters, the fuselage aft of the mid-upper turret riddled. Erks were at work between the tall twin flukes of the tail plane. Adam watched cold-eyed at Mac's shoulder for several minutes, not speaking as the erks struggled to recover the body parts from the twisted metal and shattered Perspex of the rear-turret. Little recognisably human remained of the nineteen-year-old boy gunner who had died in the turret a few hours ago, hundreds of miles from home.

The dead gunner, Jack Gresham, had been with Mac from the start.

Adam locked away his soul. Over the years he had witnessed this scene and most of its grisly variations many times. In Kassel thousands of men and women he had never met, strangers whom he would never know were pulling bodies from the rubble of their homes. Perhaps, they knew how he felt.

It never used to be such a filthy business.

"The Old Man and I have got to get off to this blasted conflab at Group," he remarked, distantly. The erks moved away from the turret as the fire hose was readied.

"Do you think the AOC will tell us anything we don't know already, sir?" Mac inquired, sourly, which was unlike him. His face was ashen. Jack Gresham's family came from the Scottish Borders. They were farmers, fine, good people, fiercely proud of their son and Jack had been their only child. Jack had been their pride and joy.

"I doubt it, Mac." Cold, grey sunlight was filtering across the wold.

Mac did not reply. Six months ago he had come to Ansham Wolds as just another sprog. In those six months his crew had become his family, the brothers he had never had. In the normal run of things crews lived and died together; when an individual was killed it was like losing a member of one's own family. Sometimes, as now, it was worse than losing a close relative. Adam understood that this was probably the darkest day of Mac's life.

He thrust his hands deeper into his greatcoat pockets, watched the erks at work. The real heroes were often the ones who had to clean up when the fighting was over. Like the erks recovering the cold meat from K-King's rear-turret. Nobody ordered them to do it; K-King was their aircraft and her crew their crew, also. They simply got on with the job. Somebody would make sure their pay books were marked up. Not that a few shillings was any recompense for performing a task no man had any right to ask another to do.

A crowd had gathered but the erks held the sightseers at bay.

An order was shouted and the fire engine's pump coughed into life. Two erks brought up the hose and directed the jet of water onto the tail assembly. The water foamed and bubbled, gushed into and out of the wrecked turret.

There was blood on the ground, now.

"I'll give you a lift back, Mac."

"I'm all right here, sir."

"I'll give you a lift back, anyway." Adam decided, gently taking the Scot by the arm. The hard edge in his voice shook Mac to his senses.

"I'm not doing much good out here. Am I?"

Gently. "No, not a lot, old man."

Chapter 31

Saturday 23rd October, 1943
No.1 Group Headquarters, Bawtry Hall, South Yorkshire

The conference was scheduled to commence at 15:00 hours. Adam and Group Captain Alexander arrived in good time and each man separately went in search of old acquaintances. Adam, prompted by a note from Pat Farlane, headed directly for the operations section.

"Your old chum the Prof's on the prowl," Pat announced as his friend walked into the office. "He was in with the Deputy AOC most of the morning."

"Oh," Adam shrugged. "Is that good or bad?"

"No idea. Nobody tells me anything." Pat frowned. "I'm only the Ops Officer, after all! Or rather, the 'acting' Ops Officer. And not that for much longer."

"No?"

"Put too many noses out of joint, old son." Pat Farlane stumped over to the window and looked out on the sprawl of Nissen huts. Half-turning, he threw Adam a thoughtful glance. "You know Freddie Tomlinson, Bill's brother? Six-Seven-Five Squadron, a good man. He takes over at the end of next week. They've promoted me Group Captain and packed me off to take command of Thirty-One OTU. For my sins. Let that be a warning to you!"

Adam took this in. Freddie Tomlinson was indeed a good man. Some ten years older than most of the Group's Squadron Commanders he had taken over 675 Squadron the week before Adam had gone to 647 Squadron at Waltham Grange. Freddie was very much a press on merchant, solid, dependable, a very safe pair of hands.

"Bit sudden?" He replied, deadpan.

"That's the way it goes, old man. I suspect the AOC woke up one morning and decided he wanted a true believer in charge of his ops section. So it goes."

Adam tried to lighten the atmosphere.

"Where the hell's Thirty-One OTU, Pat?"

"Northumberland."

"Very scenic."

"So everybody tells me!"

Adam dug out a cigarette and perched on the edge of Pat's desk.

"I'm sorry if I've given you grief the last few weeks."

The older man chuckled.

"I'll be all right. At least I'll get some flying time under my belt, again. Things could be worse."

Things could indeed be much, much worse. The one universal certainty of life in Bomber Command was that things could always get worse.

"About the Prof," Pat declared, changing the subject and depositing himself heavily in the chair behind his desk. "The Deputy AOC has a bee in his bonnet about each Group operating as an entity in its own right. You know, with an independent Pathfinder Force and Ops Staff. The AOC's given him a fair bit of leeway. Perhaps, I should say, a fair bit of rope. You know, enough to hang himself with. Like a clot I've got myself caught in the middle but between you and me I don't think my face ever really fitted around here. Anyway, I wouldn't be surprised if the Prof's doing a bit of politicking so watch your back, old man. He's probably had you in his sights ever since that spat with his people down at Waltham Grange."

Adam lit his cigarette. Said nothing.

"By God, we gave Kassel a good pasting last night," Pat went on, cheerfully, reading nothing amiss into his friend's silence. "All your aircraft got back safely, I gather?"

"More or less." Adam tried not to think about the mortal remains of Mac's rear gunner being hosed out of his wrecked turret. "Do we have the numbers for last night yet?"

"Seventeen Lancs and twenty-five Halifaxes missing. One Lanc ditched on the way back, another Lanc and a couple of Halifaxes destroyed in crashes. Six percent of the Lancaster Force, eleven percent of the Halifaxes lost. Not good. Still, it's looking like we can scratch Kassel off the target list, what!"

Adam joined Group Captain Alexander in the Great Hall of the old mansion a few minutes before the hour appointed for the commencement of the AOC's pep talk.

"Buck up, my boy," the Group Captain said, gruffly. "It seems the AOC is mightily chuffed about last night's show."

Adam wondered if the surviving crews of the Halifax Force felt as 'chuffed' as the AOC of the all-Lancaster No. 1 Group did in the aftermath of their latest decimation. "I'm glad to hear it, sir," he returned without enthusiasm.

"Dear me. What's got into you?"

"Nothing, sir. Tired, that's all. These affairs are a complete waste of time."

Alexander shook his head. "Well, be a good chap and try to keep that under your hat."

"Of course, sir."

Presently, the Group Commander made his stately entrance. The grey, stooped figure of Professor Merry was prominent in the ranks of a stage party which included the Group Senior Air Staff Officer, and all the section heads. Significantly, Pat Farlane was relegated to the back of the pack. The AOC stepped up to the lectern.

"At ease, gentlemen." He paused while his Station and Squadron Commanders settled in their seats beneath the lofty, hammer-beamed ceiling.

Adam sat down, stifling a yawn.

"Well, gentlemen," the AOC declared, "it's been quite a year." His voice carried to every corner of the Hall.

"Great deeds have been done and there are greater deeds yet to be done." As he spoke he scanned the faces of his commanders. In the same way the Chief had hand-picked him to command the Group, most of the men in the audience were his personal nominees. He trusted his commanders and in the main, they trusted him. Bomber Command was a close-knit community, a family for all the ravages of the years of war.

"Since March we have wrecked the Ruhr. We have razed Hamburg. We have burned the hearts out of many of the large cities of central and northern Germany. Shortly, we shall be going after the more distant cities, and Berlin itself."

Adam listened with half an ear. These monthly conferences, at which the AOC delivered words of wisdom and awarded miscellaneous brownie points to the worthy, invariably involved a deal of rabble rousing.

"The next few months will be decisive," the Group Commander was saying. "Gentlemen, it is within our grasp to knock Germany over by the spring by bombing alone. Gentlemen, I say to you today that the *main aim* is within our grasp!"

Adam retreated into the circle of his thoughts.

'The *main aim*.' Bomber Command's main aim had been handed down to it in its definitive form shortly before the Main Force had embarked on the systematic destruction of the Ruhr in March. The *Pointblank Directive* agreed between Churchill and Roosevelt at the Casablanca Conference in January, stated that henceforth the *main aim* of the Allied strategic bomber forces was: '*the progressive destruction and dislocation of the German military, industrial and economic system, and the undermining of the morale of the German people to a point where their capacity for armed resistance is fatally weakened.*' The 8th United States Army Air Force interpreted this to mean the precision bombing of military and industrial targets by day. To Bomber

Command the main aim had never signified anything so prosaic as a shopping list of targets to be bombed. Bomber Command's *main aim* had always been to wreck Germany from end to end: the *Pointblank Directive* was no more or less than a licence to discharge that sacred trust.

After four years of war Bomber Command was a closed and secret society united by its travails, loyal to its own in its own ways. The bomber barons were not uncaring ogres. Far from it. However, as the feudal chieftains of Bomber Command Country surveyed the monochrome prints of the unimaginable carnage on the ground, the *main aim* beckoned seductively like the lure of some latter-day Holy Grail.

The guardian, both temporal and secular, of the *main aim* was Air Chief-Marshall Sir Arthur Harris, since February 1942, Air Officer Commanding-in-Chief, RAF, Bomber Command. Adam was a rarity among operational aircrew because he had not only met, but served with the Chief. In January he had been posted to the Chief's personal staff at Bomber Command Headquarters outside High Wycombe in Buckinghamshire. To most of its huge staff High Wycombe was a dreary, pedestrian posting. People tended to work in a vacuum, minding their own business, divorced from and in some ways indifferent – in a few cases, oblivious - to the consequences of the appalling violence shaped by the select few senior officers in their midst.

The AOC was in full flow, reprising the month's successes and failures, giving credit where credit was due and highlighting the deficiencies which he confidently expected his commanders to address with the utmost urgency.

"The Hanover operation on the night of the eighth was particularly successful," he reported, warming to his sermon. "As a result of the concentrated nature of the bombing the city's telephone system and power supplies were disrupted within minutes of the commencement of the raid. Allied to the widespread disruption of a large number of water and gas mains, the city's civil defence organisation was unable to substantially inhibit the numerous fires which thereafter, swiftly developed in the central and south-central districts of Hanover. The attack overwhelmed the city's defences and serves as a classic model of a successful area attack. The marking was spot on, the Main Force bombing effort was concentrated, and creep back was negligible. In the end the city's civil defence force had no option but to fashion ad hoc firebreaks with explosives and to allow the main areas of conflagration to burn themselves out."

Nobody on the squadrons cared overmuch for the reasons why. The reasons why were secondary. *Why* was incidental. *How* was life and death. While the top brass clung to their elegant strategies the crews knuckled down to the dirty, bloody business of knocking the stuffing out of Germany. The crews cared little for the *main aim* even if the bombing of the cities was all they knew. Night after night their aiming points were situated in the middle of heavily built-up urban areas, hardly ever a specific factory, more often a cathedral or the market square of the wooden *Altstadt* of some ancient, medieval city. Schoolboy innocence soon died. The name of the game was to identify the spot markers, drop the bombs and get home in one piece. The crews understood that they were being ordered to indiscriminately bomb the civilian populations of the cities and only a tiny minority balked at it.

The Chief, *Bomber Harris* to the public, more affectionately *'Butch'* to his crews – the Germans called him *Butcher Harris* but it was not as if Hitler and his dreadful crowd had any claim to the moral high ground after Guernica, Warsaw, Rotterdam, Coventry and murdering thousands of Londoners in the Blitz - had decreed that the bombing of the cities on the plain was necessary, and more importantly, convinced the crews that it was the best way to win the war quickly. And this was enough. The crews understood that for all his bravado and bluster, the Chief was anything but a law unto himself. His orders came straight from the Allied High Command and if his superiors entertained qualms about the bombing they could, at any time, redefine the *main aim*. Until then, Bomber Command would pursue the *main aim* to its logical conclusion and history would record the razing of much of Kassel as no more than a signpost on the road to its fulfilment.

"Now, Kassel," declared the Group Commander, with a triumphal flourish. "Preliminary reports indicate that at least fifty percent of the built up area of the town was totally destroyed during the course of this morning's attack."

Adam shut his eyes. Less than thirty minutes into the attack and from four miles high it had seemed to him as if the whole city was burning. The heat from the fires had touched O-Orange, buffeted her. They had flown home from Germany with the stench of death in their nostrils. The same dreadful stench he remembered so well from Hamburg. Like Hamburg, Kassel was an object lesson in the efficacy of area bombing; or rather, what happened when the Main Force 'got it right on the night'.

Kassel could now be added to the lengthening list of German cities classified as 'having suffered a degree of damage greater than anything which we have experienced'. Berlin was not yet on that list, the wounds inflicted on London during the Blitz as yet dwarfing the retribution the RAF had exacted on the Big City. But Berlin's time would come. Soon now.

The AOC did not speculate on the date the Main Force would be set loose on Berlin. If Adam was a betting man – he was not and would never be – he would have wagered the campaign would begin around the middle of November, three weeks hence. Had the Chief meant to go to the Big City before the end of the current moonless period, he would not have risked the entire Lancaster Force against three distant, dangerous targets like Hanover, Leipzig and Kassel in the last five days.

Adam ached for a cigarette.

"Your crews must be ready to attack the most distant and heavily defended cities," the Group Commander cautioned, sternly. "Magdeburg, Brunswick, Leipzig, the cities of the eastern Baltic, Stettin and Konigsberg."

Adam did not like the sound of Konigsberg. Konigsberg was at the end of the known world in terms of a Lancaster's extreme operating range. Perhaps, the AOC was thinking of somewhere else. What on earth was there to bomb in Konigsberg, anyway?

"In the south we have Stuttgart, Frankfurt, Munich and of course, the spiritual home of the Nazis, Nuremburg."

The number of major undamaged cities beyond the Ruhr was dwindling fast. When the larger cities were burned out, the Main Force would turn on the smaller ones for that, after all, was the inescapable logic of the *main aim.*

"The main offensive will turn on Berlin," the AOC went on, stating the patently obvious. "We must wreck Berlin by the spring. Nobody should underestimate the magnitude of this task, but God-willing, we shall succeed. The critical factor will, as always, be concentration over the target."

Adam sat up and paid attention. Something had triggered his old lag's sixth sense. Suddenly he was wide awake, ears pricked, alert to danger.

"In order to maximise the effects of whatever concentration of effort we are able to achieve over the target in the coming months," the Group Commander announced, ominously, "which is unlikely to be as great over Berlin as we have achieved in some raids recently against less distant and less heavily defended targets, your aircraft will be modified so as to increase their bomb lift. Further to this end, the maximum all-up take-off weights of all Lancaster Is and IIIs will be increased from sixty-three thousand pounds to sixty-five thousand pounds. Depending on operational circumstances this figure may be subject to further incremental increases which will be advised in due course."

Adam listened with mounting horror.

"I shall not go into details at this stage," the AOC commented. "However, in essence, the modifications to your aircraft will involve the removal of all armour plate, excepting that directly behind the pilot's position." He was oblivious to the sharp intakes of breath this news occasioned. "The nett result of these modifications, taken in conjunction with the increased all-up take-off weights I have authorised, will be to increase your Lancasters' bomb lift by around three thousand pounds, or to permit your aircraft to carry an extra four hundred gallons of fuel."

The news was greeted with stony silence. Most of the Squadron Commanders in the room could already hear the distant thunderclaps of cookies splashing into the North Sea. All the way from the Humber Estuary to the Zuider Zee! When the conference ended the room emptied, quietly, thoughtfully into the Mess.

"Two large gins!" Group Captain Alexander demanded, taking his Wing-Commander to one side in the scrum. "This won't go down well with the crews!"

"No, sir," Adam was bound to agree. The crews would feel betrayed and they had every right to feel betrayed. Inevitably, some men would take matters into their own hands, and attempt to redress the odds by lightening their loads before they crossed the enemy coast. Other Squadron Commanders would be hurriedly following his example and wiring up the camera release mechanism to each aircraft's cookie.

"I've half a mind to put in a formal protest," the Group Captain seethed.

"With respect, I don't think that would be a very good idea, sir."

"It's a disgrace!"

Adam shrugged. Whether or not it was 'a disgrace' was a moot point. The AOC had spoken and for better or worse they were going to have to make the best of a bad deal and get on with it.

"Excuse me, sir. Time to mingle." Catching sight of Pat Farlane he waved and detached himself from his Station Commander.

"My, my," remarked his friend. "I was beginning to wonder if I'd been sent to Coventry."

"It wasn't your idea, was it?"

"The armour and the increased take-off weights?" Pat retorted. "No, not me, old man. You don't think I'd be off to Northumberland if I was the sort of chap who'd come up with a spiffing wheeze like that!"

"Sorry."

"Bit of a corker though, what?"

Adam downed his gin. "As you know, some of my Lancs have been operating at take-off weights of sixty-five thousand pounds," he said, lowly. "The problem's not getting airborne, it's gaining altitude before you get to the enemy coast. My old lags are okay flying at these weights. But it's no good for sprogs."

"Not much is these days, old son."

"Adam Chantrey!" A familiar, oddly strained voice called.

"Looks like the Prof's got you in his sights," Pat warned. "I'd corkscrew port, if I were you."

"Too low, old man," Adam grimaced. "I'd go straight into the deck!"

"In that case you'll have to stay and take your medicine, then."

Adam steeled himself, and turned to face Eleanor's father. Professor Merry smiled as he struggled through the press of bodies. Stopping a yard in front of the younger man, he ran his eye over him.

"Congratulations on the Bar to your D.S.O., Chantrey."

"Thank you, sir."

"No need to be so defensive, my boy. I've learned my lesson. My business with the Deputy AOC concerns our Antipodean friends over at Binbrook. I won't be stepping on your toes again. Rest assured, Ansham Wolds is safe."

Adam relaxed a fraction.

"I don't suppose there's any possibility of having that in writing, sir?"

The Professor laughed but Adam kept his guard high, reflexes primed. The Prof justified his caution almost immediately.

"What's this I hear about your old lags operating at take-off weights of sixty-five thousand pounds for the last three weeks?"

Adam would not be drawn.

The Prof went on. "Nothing like testing a theory under operational conditions? You know, to find out what's what? What works and what doesn't? I gather the AOC's been itching to give this a go for some time, now. Then along you come and give it a try; and prove it can be done without scattering Lancasters all over the wolds. Of course, if any of your aircraft had crashed you'd have been for the high jump."

"Possibly, sir." The 'high jump' was putting it a bit strongly. To the best of his knowledge nobody had even been taken to task in Bomber Command for pressing on *too much*. The old man's stare had fixed on him.

"Not that it was about proving it could be done," the

Prof acknowledged. "You already knew it could be done. You'd already flown Lancasters at much higher all-up weights at Boscombe Down, of course. I suspect it was your way of telling the people at Group that 647 Squadron was on the mend?"

"I think you give me too much credit, sir." Adam forced a smile.

Professor Merry saw at last the anger simmering beneath the younger man's veneer of respectful amiability. Too late he recognised the deep weariness in his eyes, the greyness in his face. That the younger man was exhausted, operating on the shortest of short leashes.

"I take it you were over Kassel last night?"

"Old lag's party," Adam said, enigmatically. He saw Group Captain Alexander looking in his direction. "Excuse me, sir."

Professor Merry watched him go. "Old lag's party, indeed," he muttered to himself. The Mess was emptying around him. The AOC, having made a token appearance, had delegated his duties as host to his deputy, and departed. The Group Commander was not a social animal and rarely pretended otherwise. The Professor found a chair, sat down, glad of the opportunity to catch his breath. The effect of his pills wore off too quickly. Quicker day by day. He had mishandled his conversation with young Chantrey. Instead of making his peace with the boy he had antagonised him, and diminished himself in his eyes. What would have been the harm in telling the boy that he was at Bawtry to tie up a few loose ends? That his visit to Binbrook was no more than a courtesy call, his swansong. The trouble was that lying, that rationing out the truth in penny parcels was too ingrained. There were so many things he ought to have told Eleanor; but knew now he never would.

"A medicinal sherry, Charles," suggested the Deputy

AOC, Air Commodore Crowe-Martin, interrupting his reverie, pressing a glass into his hands, and sitting down opposite him by the window. Outside the dusk was coming down mistily. "One won't do any harm. I don't care what your doctor says."

"Thank you. What shall we drink to, Stephen?"

"Absent friends."

The Professor sipped his sherry, happily savouring the forbidden fruit of the vine.

"So, the AOC thinks we can knock the Germans over this winter." He prompted, glumly. The Group Commander believed that victory was within Bomber Command's grasp; and because he believed it he was prepared to push his crews to the absolute limit of their courage and endurance. "What do you think, Stephen?"

Crowe-Martin made no attempt to dissemble.

"I honestly don't know if we can knock the Bosch out of the war by bombing alone, Charles." He was gazing out of the window. "It is a possibility, certainly. A few more nights like last night and who knows?"

Professor Merry had once been one of the faithful, a true-believer. Two years ago he had preached that the unrestricted bombing of the German cities was the only alternative to a repetition of the tragedy of the trenches in the last war. Now as his life ebbed away and the great offensive gathered a terrible unstoppable momentum old doubts had re-surfaced. If the photographic record of the devastation in the Ruhr and elsewhere in Germany was incontrovertible; so too was the fact that Germany's capacity to wage war seemed undiminished. Increasingly, the extravagant claims made by the disciples of the *main aim* struck a discordant note. As death approached his faith had deserted him.

"I'm sorry, Stephen," he apologised, slowly. "Even if I believed we could do to Berlin what we did to Kassel last night, and I have profound reservations on that score, I can't help but think back to our own experience in forty and forty-one."

"Oh?"

"If anything the bombing was a force for national unity. There's a school of thought in the Air Ministry which maintains that even if we destroyed every German city, there's no guarantee that the Germans would be any more inclined to roll over than they are now. Do you remember the expedients we were driven to in the Blitz? Shadow factories, the large-scale dispersal and duplication of vital industrial processes, the mass evacuation of civilians from the big cities. We've not been under sustained attack since forty-one, imagine the lengths we'd have been driven to if we'd been taking the kind of punishment the Ruhr has taken this last year."

Crowe-Martin leaned forward.

"I agree with everything you're saying. However, aren't you forgetting the main thing?"

The Professor frowned. "The massive scale of our attacks," the Deputy AOC continued, "is of a completely different order of magnitude to that which we experienced in the Blitz. When we go to Berlin we shall be dropping five to ten times more bombs in a single night than the Luftwaffe dropped in the worst raids of the London Blitz. Our whole bombing policy is founded on the assumption that the immense dislocation caused by the great weight of our attacks, will inevitably render impossible any widespread dispersal and re-organisation of the German war effort."

"Desperate situations tend to bring forth desperate remedies, Stephen," the older man objected.

His friend smiled.

"Either way," he said, "I suspect it's a little late in the day to be playing Devil's Advocate, old chap."

Chapter 32

Saturday 30th October, 1943
Boultham, Lincoln, Lincolnshire

In two days – less than two days now - Suzy was due to depart for Shrewsbury.

That afternoon the innocents had driven down to Lincoln and fetched up in a truly 'horrid little back room' in not so much 'the middle of nowhere', as on the shabbier, most neglected side of the city. They were quietly terrified. Their adventure was fraught with pitfalls, neither of them really knew what they were doing or how they were supposed to behave and most frightening of all, it was all so new.

Although the room was grubby and had not seen a new coat of paint in years, it was warm. Or rather, marginally on the warm side of cold. A few glowing coals smoked in the small first floor hearth and the air was damp, musty.

Suzy tried her best to put a brave face on things. She drew the curtains and looked to the man.

"Here we are, then?"

"I'm sorry," Peter Tilliard muttered, wishing he had sought Jack Gordon's advice. Like a fool he had not wanted to risk Suzy's ire again and as a result brought her to this dreadful hovel. "I didn't expect it to be this horrid."

"It's not *that* horrid," she chided him. "Besides, it doesn't matter. We're here. Together. That's all that matters."

If he had not been so nervous he would have got down on his knees, worshipped the ground upon which she stood and kissed her feet. He held out his arms and she walked into them and leaned on him. They were both trembling.

"Aren't we a pair," she laughed, nervily.

Tilliard did not trust himself to speak.

He planted a kiss in her hair, breathed her in.

"I think we ought to lock the door," Suzy decided.

"Absolutely," he agreed.

The lock was stiff and the door frame was distorted. He put his shoulder against the door, turned the key. He tried the door handle, checked the door was securely locked. When he looked around Suzy was sitting on the bed. She smiled and patted the cover by her side. Pausing to hang his greatcoat on the peg by the door he hesitantly did as he was bade. The bed creaked loudly as if each spring in the ancient mattress was squealing in pain, the headboard which was loose, thudded against the wall. He put his arm around her shoulders.

They kissed, tentatively.

"You're sure about this?" He asked.

Suzy nodded, blue eyes twinkling.

"Yes, darling."

"I love you."

"And I love you."

She slid onto his lap and as they kissed she guided his right hand onto the small, firm mound of her left breast, drew him slowly down onto the bed. The bed creaked deafeningly, and the headboard struck the wall another resounding blow. They froze, looked at each other. It was impossible to say afterwards which one of them laughed first because moments later they were both laughing helplessly, tears streaming down their faces. As laughter often does, it miraculously cleansed them of their nervousness and shredded the fear that had threatened to make them strangers. They kicked off their shoes, started pulling, fumbling, struggling with their clothes, breathless and wide-eyed.

"Wait," she murmured in his ear. "You'll ladder my stockings."

Tilliard got off her. She sat up, hitched up her skirt, unclipped her grey stockings and carefully rolled each down over her thigh, knee, calf and ankle. He stared transfixed at her legs, their white perfection set against the darkness of the blanket. Shyly, avoiding his eye she unhooked her skirt, wriggled out of it. She reached for the hem of her slip, drew it slowly, deliberately to her waist, then her navel, then to her chin. He stared at her near nakedness, mesmerised.

"Make love to me," she mouthed. Discarding his tunic, tie and shirt, he moved above her. She tugged at his trousers, pushed them over his hips. "Now..."

Suzy smiled up into his face, so happily that it made the man tingle from head to toe. He felt her part her legs, spread herself wide beneath him. The inside of her knees brushed against the outside of his thighs. The touch of her bare flesh against his was more than he could endure and he plunged into her, clumsily, roughly. She gasped, moaned and clung to him, her eyes closed, her lips opened. She was so moist, warm, yielding he came almost immediately, or so it seemed, exploding within her. He collapsed on top of her, his heart racing, the blood pounding in his temples, dazed. Suzy sighed, ran her fingers up his spine, across his back, his buttocks, tickling, kneading, scratching playfully. All the while she moved under him, against him, gently prolonging the pleasure and the pain of it, holding him deep inside her, unwilling to release him or to let the moment end.

Only when the chill of the room began to sink into their bones did she relax her hold and permit him to leave her. Suzy shrugged off her bra, exposing her small, round breasts. Tilliard dragged his eyes from her, stepped out of his trousers and slid into the bed. They pulled the blankets up to their chins and lay nakedly together for the first time. When she shivered he circled her in his arms, she curled up safe in his embrace and soon, they slept.

Later, in the cold darkness her hands explored his

loins and with a long sigh, she rolled onto her back. He mounted her, took her greedily, hungrily as she lay beneath him, giggling, moaning. Again, when he was spent she wrapped herself around him, clung to him. There were tears in her eyes. Tears of happiness, tears of terror, tears for whatever awaited them in an unknowable future.

"I didn't think it would be like this?" She sniffed in the dark.

Gently, the man disentangled himself, rolled off the woman.

"I didn't know what to expect, either," he confessed, his voice urgent with concern, worried.

"I'm being silly," she muttered.

"No."

"I am. I feel so happy, so complete, but..." The man listened, saying nothing. Suzy shrugged close to him, nestled in the crook of his arm. "But I'm going away in a couple of days and I don't know when I'll see you again. Or when we'll be together again. Or when we'll do this again. It's all so unfair!"

Tilliard stroked her hair.

"I know."

Suzy lifted her face to his, kissed him slowly, open-mouthed.

Slowly, urgently she drew him down on top of her.

Chapter 33

Sunday 31st October, 1943
RAF Ansham Wolds, Lincolnshire

Throwing caution to the wind they had arranged to meet in the shadows between the Nissen huts beyond the Waafery. A frigid north wind gusted fitfully and spots of icy rain bounced off their shoulders.

"I could get pregnant," Suzy said, her face hidden in the gloom. "For all I know I could be pregnant, now," she added, calmly, thinking out aloud.

Tilliard was startled. She might indeed be pregnant. Confronting the prospect opened up a vista of possibilities, each as frightful as the next.

"If I am," she asked, bluntly, "will you marry me?"

"Of course!"

"But not unless I'm pregnant?"

In his state of high anxiety Tilliard did not realise that Suzy was teasing him. "No, that's not what I meant!"

She laughed, stood on her toes and kissed him.

"I know that's not what you meant, silly."

Booted footsteps at the end of the hut made them edge deeper into the shadows where the powerful beam of a torch found them.

"Who goes there!" Demanded the guard.

For Tilliard it was the last straw. Stepping in front of Suzy he squinted down the beam.

"Put that bloody light out!" He growled, hands on hips.

The light clicked off, instantly.

"Er, sorry, sir." The guard marched off, smartly.

"Do you think he recognised us, darling?" Suzy asked, threading her arm through the man's.

"Yes. Thank goodness!"

Not for the first time Tilliard had good reason to be

thankful the Wingco had thoroughly terrorised the Guard Flight Commander, and in the process instilled the cardinal rule that: 'in any dispute I will ALWAYS support my crews'. That was the Wingco's secret, of course. As long as a man did his best, pressed on over Germany a chap could get away with murder. Well, almost. He turned his attention back to Suzy.

"If things weren't what they are," he said, hoarsely. "I'd propose to you at the drop of a hat. You know that, don't you?"

Suzy nodded. Tomorrow she would be leaving Ansham Wolds. She might never see him again. He might be killed tomorrow. It was awful, it was unspeakably unfair but it was how things were and there was nothing either of them could do about it. Except carry with them their memories of last night, and try come what may, to cling to their hopes and to their faith in each other. She rested against him and he held her tight. Shutting her eyes she was instantly in another place, beneath him as he rocked backwards and forwards on her, inside her in the big, noisy bed in Lincoln. She had worried if she was doing the right thing but now she had no doubts. It was reckless, and it might yet be the ruin of her but had they parted without having made love, parted without having been *true lovers* she would have regretted it forever. The thought of parting without ever having lain with him, without having been one flesh with him, without ever having expressed physically and in every other way her love for him, would have surely tormented her for the rest of her life. This she understood intuitively. It was beyond infatuation, infinitely more than a girlish captivation; it was the mad flush of first love.

Tears rolled uncontrollably down her cheeks.

[The End]

Author's End Note

Thank you for reading **The Road to Berlin**. I hope you enjoyed it; if not, I am sorry. Either way, I still thank you for giving of your time and attention to read it. Civilisation depends on people like you.

Although all the events depicted in the narrative of **The Road to Berlin** are set in a specific place and time the characters in it are the constructs of my own imagination. *Ansham Wolds, Waltham Grange, Kelmington* and *Faldwell* are fictional Bomber Command bases, likewise, *380, 388* and *647 Squadrons* exist only in my head. While *Bawtry Hall* was the Headquarters of No 1 Group, I have made no attempt to accurately depict it, or any members of the command staff posted to it in 1943 and 1944. Moreover, the words and actions attributed to specific officers at Bawtry Hall and elsewhere are *my* words.

One final thought.

A note on jargon. I have been at pains to make **The Road to Berlin** accessible to readers who are relatively new to the subject matter and therefore not necessarily wholly conversant with the technologies and contemporary Royal Air Force 'service speak'; while attempting *not* to sacrifice the atmosphere and *reality* of that subject matter for readers who are already immersed in Bomber Command's campaigns. For example, I describe aircraft by employing their designated 'letters' – that is, B-Baker, or T-Tommy and so on – rather than using the common RAF parlance of referring to an aircraft by its serial number. Likewise, where possible I look to explain technical terms and procedures in layperson's language. Inevitably, this leaves one open to the charge that one is 'dumbing down'; but there are many trade-offs in writing any serious work of fiction, and I sincerely hope I have drawn the line in more or less the right place. However, this is a judgement I leave to you, my reader.

Other Books by James Philip

The Timeline 10/27/62 World

The Timeline 10/27/62 - Main Series

Book 1: Operation Anadyr

Book 2: Love is Strange

Book 3: The Pillars of Hercules

Book 4: Red Dawn

Book 5: The Burning Time

Book 6: Tales of Brave Ulysses

Book 7: A Line in the Sand

Book 8: The Mountains of the Moon

Book 9: All Along the Watchtower

Book 10: Crow on the Cradle

Book 11: 1966 & All That

A standalone Timeline10/27/62 Novel

Football In The Ruins – The World Cup of 1966

Coming in 2018-19

Book12: Only In America

Book 13: Warsaw Concerto

Timeline 10/27/62 - USA

Book 1: Aftermath

Book 2: California Dreaming

Book 3: The Great Society

Book 4: Ask Not of Your Country

Book 5: The American Dream

Timeline 10/27/62 – Australia

Book 1: Cricket on the Beach
Book 2: Operation Manna

Other Series & Books

The Guy Winter Mysteries

Prologue: Winter's Pearl
Book 1: Winter's War
Book 2: Winter's Revenge
Book 3: Winter's Exile
Book 4: Winter's Return
Book 5: Winter's Spy
Book 6: Winter's Nemesis

The Harry Waters Series

Book 1: Islands of No Return
Book 2: Heroes
Book 3: Brothers in Arms

The Frankie Ransom Series

Book 1: A Ransom for Two Roses
Book 2: The Plains of Waterloo
Book 3: The Nantucket Sleighride

The Strangers Bureau Series

Book 1: Interlopers
Book 2: Pictures of Lily

NON-FICTION CRICKET BOOKS

FS Jackson
Lord Hawke

Audio Books of the following Titles
are available (or are in production) now

Aftermath
After Midnight
A Ransom for Two Roses
Brothers in Arms
California Dreaming
Heroes
Islands of No Return
Love is Strange
Main Force Country
Operation Anadyr
The Big City
The Cloud Walkers
The Nantucket Sleighride
The Painter
The Pillars of Hercules
The Road to Berlin
The Plains of Waterloo
Until the Night
When Winter Comes
Winter's Exile
Winter's Nemesis
Winter's Pearl
Winter's Return
Winter's Revenge
Winter's Spy
Winter's War

Cricket Books edited by James Philip

The James D. Coldham Series
[Edited by James Philip]

Books

Northamptonshire Cricket: A History [1741-1958]
Lord Harris

Anthologies

Volume 1: Notes & Articles
Volume 2: Monographs No. 1 to 8

Monographs

No. 1 - William Brockwell
No. 2 - German Cricket
No. 3 - Devon Cricket
No. 4 - R.S. Holmes
No. 5 - Collectors & Collecting
No. 6 - Early Cricket Reporters
No. 7 – Northamptonshire
No. 8 - Cricket & Authors

————

Details of all James Philip's books and forthcoming
publications
will be found on his website www.jamesphilip.co.uk

Cover artwork concepts by James Philip
Graphic Design by Beastleigh Web Design

Printed in Great Britain
by Amazon

84766887R00140